D0435613

# Payment for Silence

ANNE RIVERS

# *Payment for Silence*

**WALKER AND COMPANY**
New York

Copyright © Anne Rivers 1974
All rights reserved. No part of this book may be reproduced or
transmitted in any form or by any means, electronic or
mechanical, including photocopying, recording, or by any
information storage and retrieval system, without permission in writing
from the Publisher.
All the characters and events
portrayed in this story are fictitious.
First published in the United States of America in 1975 by
the Walker Publishing Company, Inc.

ISBN: 0-8027-5300-0

Library of Congress Catalog Card Number: 73-93931

Printed in the United States of America.

10   9   8   7   6   5   4   3   2   1

To Maria Greatly it all began when she glanced up from her deckchair and saw her daughter Clare and a strange young man walking across the grass together.

She would never forget that moment. For some reason she was immediately uneasy. And from then on the uneasiness grew, not dramatically, but steadily wearing away the smooth fabric of all their lives until one dark, dangerous night a whole new pattern was created.

The very appearance of the couple was like a well-staged theatrical entrance. It was in fact difficult *not* to make a theatrical entrance, in the circumstances. The Greatlys' house, King's View, though not large, was old, beautiful and set like a small, perfect gem, in a background of superb simplicity. Facing the sea but set well back, there was nothing between it and the cliff edge but a sweep of short springy turf. If you sat, as Maria and her friends did now, in the middle of this magnificent and wholly natural lawn, you had a view of the sea to your right where the cliff had fallen away; while to the left was the tree-lined zig-zag path down to the hidden beach. Or you could look inland to the house and the wide drive that ran round from the back to the old stables, now a garage, at the side.

It was from the stables that Clare and the stranger now approached and even as she was filled with that unaccountable premonition of disaster, Maria was also able to enjoy the spectacle of almost unbelievable good looks.

Few men were tall enough to tower over Clare. Even her fiancé was only an inch or so taller. But this young man could give her four or five inches. It was Clare's height, plus the fact that classic blonde beauty was no longer fashionable, that had put her at the age of twenty-six into the second rank of models, rather than at their head. But viewed unprofessionally as an ornament to a summer afternoon, she could hardly have been bettered. And the man beside her, tanned, blue-eyed, his hair a fashionable length but unquestionably groomed, was as handsome as she was beautiful. And yet Maria had this odd feeling that all was not well.

'Mother!' Maria was always amused at the way in which Clare's manner belied her looks. Impulsive and uncalculating, she swiftly acknowledged the friends surrounding her mother and went, as usual, straight to the matter that was on her mind. 'Where is Stuart?'

Maria wondered fleetingly why she should be expected to account for a man who, although a friend and close neighbour, was not her personal charge. But she was used to Clare and she answered without rancour.

'I don't know. I rang up to ask him over to tea but he must have been out.'

'Well it's very odd. This is Michael Highstone and he's supposed to be staying at Port King for the weekend but Stu's not at home and the house is empty.'

6

Maria and Michael murmured their how do you do's, and Maria introduced her guests.

She felt faintly sorry for Michael who was undoubtedly getting a rather more than polite appraisal from her party. His extraordinary good looks, the relaxed moment of the day at which he had so unexpectedly arrived, and his unusual situation as a guest without a host put him somewhat at the mercy of a group ready for a diversion. He took it, however, in his elegant stride and explained his position with good humour.

'I should have telephoned to make sure all was well but I couldn't get to a phone last night and since I'd received a letter from Stuart confirming our plans, I took it to be all right.'

'He may have gone into Tormouth to do some shopping,' Maria said. 'His manservant is away and Stuart has been looking after himself.'

'Except for the rough. Mrs. Tresimmon has been going in every day to do that,' said Jill Tredger, wife of the local solicitor and an old friend of Maria's. 'She passes my house every morning on her way to Port King. Dear old witch,' she added, affectionately. 'Where shall we be when they all die out?'

'If, as I take it, the old witch goes in daily to work for Stuart, would she know if I am expected?' asked Michael.

'Yes, she probably would,' Maria felt it was time to take charge of the situation. 'But why don't you sit down and have a cup of tea? Probably Stuart got delayed in Tormouth; or he might even have had to go further. In a little while we'll ring Port King again.'

'Could he be on the Rock?' said John Tredger suddenly.

Instinctively all but Michael turned their heads towards the sea. It was a useless gesture for the Rock was not visible from here. A small circular island, it lay so close to the mainland that it could only be seen from the cliff edge.

Clare had stretched herself out on the grass, and invited Michael to join her. Now she said lazily, 'Here comes Penny. She may know. She's been down to the beach.'

Still in her mood of detached watchfulness, Maria noted her niece's entrance with interest. Whereas Clare and Michael had moved quite slowly and with infinite grace towards the group on the lawn, Penny's progress was erratic, partly due to the brown mongrel that circled round her, making a mile of every metre. Her wild hair burnt a red hole in the shimmering air. She wore a swimsuit—a suit for swimming in, thought Maria, amused, quite unlike any of Clare's exotic little strips of fabric. On her feet were old espadrilles which, combined with the spring of the turf, made her progress towards the scene both silent and beautiful. Her legs were lovely, Maria thought suddenly, better than Clare's even. Pity she's top heavy, maybe it's just puppy fat. On the other hand, she reflected, perhaps it's attractive. She looked at Michael to see if he had reacted to her long-legged, top-heavy niece but Michael was looking at Clare. Maria, feeling uneasy again, turned back to watch Penny.

Ever since Maria's brother and his doctor wife had gone to work in China ten years before, Penny Keats had made King's View her home. She looked

8

upon Maria as a second mother and Clare as an older sister, and though the two girls were as different in character as they were in looks, their relationship had been one of unclouded affection. And for this Maria had her own reasons to be thankful. If the two girls had not got on life could have been very complicated indeed. Now, as so often in the past, she felt that Penny would probably put things into proportion and that her own uneasiness would soon be allayed.

The dog carefully calculated its circling so that it arrived by the tea table at the same time as Penny. She, punctilious as her cousin was casual, greeted everyone, even putting out a strong brown hand to shake Michael's carefully manicured one when Clare introduced them.

'He's not on the Rock; the boat's in the inlet,' Penny said briefly, when asked about Stuart. 'Come to think of it I haven't seen him since the day before yesterday.'

'Maybe he's going to swim back,' said John.

Penny shook her head. 'He never does that.'

'No, if the boat's here, he's on the mainland.' Clare was unexpectedly definite.

'Unless he used Blanes' boat.'

'He'd only do that if there was something wrong with his own. And there isn't. Or there wasn't, yesterday. I borrowed it.' Penny caught her aunt's eye. 'With Stuart's permission.'

'What is the Rock?' asked Michael. 'And why does Stuart go to it?'

'You can fish there for one thing,' Penny sat down on the grass and poured some milk for Susie the dog

9

who now lay complaining about the long walk she'd been forced to take.

'It's *his*,' explained Clare. 'He's King of the island, and he goes to survey his domain.'

'Heavens, I'd no idea he was such a romantic figure, I only knew him through his boat-building business.'

'You're honoured. Stuart doesn't usually mix his business and private lives.' Clare looked at him with fresh curiosity. *Why you*? was going to be the next question Maria thought wildly, and for some reason she felt she had to prevent it. But before she could speak John Tredger moved the conversation on.

'Where's Clive, Clare? I thought he was supposed to be on holiday with you.'

'He was.' Clare turned her exquisite face to the sky and blinked at the sun. 'But the poor old boy had to work on a few days. He'll be here soon.' She raised her arm and squinted at her watch against the strong light. 'Any minute now, I should think.'

'What *is* his job exactly?' asked another of Maria's guests suddenly. 'I don't believe I've ever known.'

There was a moment's silence, then Clare turned to the speaker with a smile. 'He's a civil servant, Rowena,' she said blandly. 'Pretty dull really, but he works very hard.'

Maria felt a little sorry for her daughter. It must be maddening to know your fiancé was a high-ranking trouble-shooter for a very secret government department and have to keep quiet about it. The temptation to boast a little must be considerable, particularly to someone like Rowena Carter whose husband was known to be a highly successful businessman. She wondered if Rowena suspected some subterfuge on Clare's part but Rowena's rather lovely face appeared to be quite innocent.

'Didn't Clive have an accident recently?' Jill Tredger asked. 'Is he over it?'

'He's had *everything* lately,' Clare said. 'First flu, and then he smashed his car and hurt his foot, and then he got German measles of all unlikely things. And by the time that was over, he'd got such a conscience about his work that he delayed his holiday for a couple of weeks.'

'And then his dog died,' said Penny.

Maria looked at her niece and smiled. 'Yes, poor Clive. He could have done without that.'

'Never mind, we'll give him a good time once he's here.' Clare rolled over and then sat up suddenly. 'Talk of the devil—here he is.'

Once again Maria was conscious of an entrance— an entrance on cue this time, with the audience prepared for the new character. A sympathetic audience, she felt, one that had been gently stirred by the tale of woe so lightly recounted by Clare, so oddly climaxed by Penny.

He looked to Maria's heightened senses like a man to whom all those things had happened and more as well; a man striving to appear cheerful, and in holiday mood, against all odds.

His looks were of the fair and unassuming kind that were dependent on his mood and physical well-being. They were not at their best today and Maria noted with a sinking heart that the resultant comparison with the hale and cheerful Michael was not flattering to him.

Well, she thought, he had been ill—more ill per-

11

haps than Clare had indicated. But now he was here he would quickly recover his looks and his spirits.

Clare had risen to greet him and even now as he put his arm round her the grimness in his face was replaced by his disarming smile. And though he was nowhere near as handsome as Michael and at least five years older he moved with equal and less calculated grace. And his faint aloofness made the other man's open, candid manner seem a little naïve.

My goodness thought Maria suddenly, he's precious to me; nothing must happen to him. Clare, she begged inwardly, be good to him, he deserves the best.

He turned to her now and kissed her affectionately before he shook hands all round, greeted the ecstatic Susie and patted Penny's small, neat behind. 'Nice to see you, doctor,' he said.

'Only two more years to go and you can take the silly grin off your face when you say that.'

'Go on, I don't believe you. You're a baby.'

'A brilliant one,' Penny said. 'That's what you forget.'

Yes we do, thought Maria. While Clare gathers the glances, Penny passes the exams. One day she will be a force to be reckoned with, I must remember that. She stored the thought away for future consideration, and turned back to Clive who had flung himself down on the grass.

'What was the journey like?'

'Awful. My own fault. I should have started earlier.'

'Bad luck, love.' Clare patted his shoulder. 'Michael said the roads were quite clear and he was only an hour in front of you.'

Clive grunted. 'I'm surprised, they looked as if

they'd been clogged for ever. Perhaps he knows some quiet ways.'

Michael smiled. 'Not as many as you do, I'm sure. It's unfamiliar country to me. But an hour or so can make a lot of difference.'

'True. If you pick the wrong hour, you can make two hours difference. I never understand that; it seems to me to be mathematically impossible.' He sighed and closed his eyes. 'Well I'm here now.'

'Would you like some tea, Clive?' Maria bent over and removed the dog, Susie, who was about to give Clive's face a good wash. 'Or a drink? Or a bath? Or a sleep?'

'No thanks.' The brilliant grey eyes opened suddenly. 'A swim, that's what I'd like. And then a drink. O.K.? Come with me, Clare?'

'Darling, I was swimming all the morning, and now I've had my hair done in your honour. Sorry.'

He put his hand gently on top of her shining head, 'And it looks gorgeous. I shan't be long.'

There was then a half-hearted attempt on the part of the tea-guests to gather themselves together and go home but Maria stopped them.

'How often can we just sit in the sun like this? Let's do it while we can. Clare and I will take the tea things in, Michael can phone Stuart while we get some drinks.'

Michael rose immediately and began to pack the china on to a tray.

In the kitchen, Clare said to her mother: 'Suppose Stuart isn't there? Can we give Michael dinner?'

'Of course we can. But Stuart will be there. He doesn't forget things.'

Michael came in wearing a puzzled frown. 'There's

13

still no reply. I think I should go and call on Mrs. What is it—Tresimmon?'

Maria stopped with a bottle in her hand and thought carefully.

'Blanes is expected home tonight. We could leave a message for him at the house.'

'Blanes is . . .?'

'Stuart's manservant.' Clare grinned. 'He's a real lord of the manor, you know, our Stuart.'

'I didn't know.' Michael looked confused. 'I really know very little about him.'

'He's hardly Lord of the Manor now,' said Maria briskly. 'But his ancestors certainly were. They lived on the Rock in solitary splendour in a wicked old castle that is now blessedly uninhabitable. So Stuart lives at Port King on the mainland below the cliff. Blanes went to work at Port King when he was a boy and has been there ever since.'

'Alone? He never married?'

'Stuart didn't. Blanes did but his wife died, which is why he stayed in the same place for so long. Luckily for Stuart he can do no wrong in Blanes' eyes so he's never lacked comfort. And Blanes will be back tonight as planned, and explain everything, I don't doubt. Meanwhile you can spend the evening with us.'

She felt that hospitality and her long friendship with Stuart King demanded this much. But she wished she knew more about this young man who seemed himself to know so little about Stuart. The uneasiness persisted though she could not fault him. His manners were as good as his looks, he seemed genuinely diffident about imposing himself on her.

'Where did you meet him?' she asked Clare when

14

Michael had gone ahead of them carrying a tray of drinks out to the lawn.

'I found him wandering about Stuart's house, looking for someone. I was coming up from the beach.'

There were two ways up from the beach to the cliff top; one the zig-zag path that belonged to the Greatlys and the other a longer, gently rising lane through Stuart's grounds. But Greatlys and Kings used each other's rights of way by agreement. Clare would have no sense of trespassing when she met Michael at Port King: but she might have thought that Michael was trespassing. It was clear however that it had never occurred to her. She had simply offered to help. Well, we shall see, Maria thought, following her daughter across the grass. Either Stuart will turn up or Blanes will.

The blazing afternoon was turning imperceptibly into golden evening. The deckchairs had been turned round towards the sun, now glinting on the silver line of the sea beyond the broken cliff edge. Penny had made a concession to the arrival of drinks by pulling a pair of shorts and a shirt over her swimsuit. Susie had disappeared and Clive was presumably still wallowing in the cove below them.

'If only it could always be like this.' Rowena Carter accepted a drink from Clare and sat back with a contented sigh. 'But I suppose tomorrow it will be raining,' she glanced at her watch. 'Ten minutes and then I must go. George will be home this evening.'

George, as far as Maria knew, very rarely *was* home. He was still regarded in the village as a newcomer for he and Rowena had been in the neighbourhood only two years and for most of that time

15

Rowena had been alone in her big beautiful house above the harbour. She had never complained of loneliness but Maria had felt sorry for her and made some efforts to introduce her to local people. She was friendly enough and so was George—if you could ever get friendly with a man who always appeared to be on the verge of leaving for somewhere else. Not for the first time Maria felt obscurely sorry for Rowena Carter.

In the distance Susie began to bark, the sound carrying nearer and nearer as she reached the top of the zig-zag. There she stopped, obviously waiting.

Clive came slowly at first, Susie, quiet now, at his heels.

Another entrance thought Maria and the uneasy feeling was with her again.

'John,' Clive addressed himself to the solicitor without preamble, 'I need help on the beach. I've found Stuart in the water.'

There was a moment's paralysed silence. So this is it, thought Maria and put down her glass with what seemed an astonishing amount of noise.

Penny got to her feet.

'Alive?' she asked.

'Dead?' said Rowena Carter at the same moment.

'Yes, I'm afraid so.' Clive answered Rowena. 'I managed to get him on to the beach but we need a stretcher. An ambulance.'

'The police too.' John Tredger stood up. 'I'll phone.'

'Put your head between your knees,' said Penny to Rowena. She turned to Clive. 'I'll get down there, you go with John.'

'No, you can't, I'll go back in a moment.'

'How long . . . ?' asked Penny.

'Hours,' he said briefly.

Maria poured a whisky and gave it to Clive. 'Have him brought here,' he said.

'No.' Clive spoke sharply. 'We'll take him to Port King. Maria, did you say the house is empty?'

'Till—yes—it must be. Blanes won't be home till later tonight.'

'Don't you have a key?'

'Yes. I'll get it.' Clare started for the house.

'I must get back to the cove.' Clive drained his drink and put down his glass with a steady hand.

'I'll come with you,' said Penny.

'No. There's nothing you can do.'

'I'm coming.'

'No.'

She looked at him then, studying his face intently. 'Get your trousers and a shirt on,' she said. 'You may begin to feel inadequately dressed when the police come.'

'I'll come to the beach with you.' Michael was very pale and made the offer with an obvious effort. But, thought Maria, he did make it, I'll try to remember that.

'No, thanks. But perhaps you'd go with Clare to Port King, in case—in case they bring Stuart there before I get there.'

'Right.' Michael went after Clare, managing to make his relief not too apparent.

A few minutes later Clive, more adequately clothed, reached the bottom of the zig-zag and crossed the beach to the rocks on to which he had dragged Stuart. Penny was sitting on a flat rock, her hands clasped round her knees, her bright head drooping. She looked up as he approached.

'I told you not to come,' he said.

'Poor old Stu,' she said. 'Poor harmless old Stuart.'

'You've seen him.'

'Of course.'

'His head . . .'

'Instantaneous, I should think. No wonder you didn't want him taken up to King's View. What do you think happened?'

'I suppose the tide flung him on the rocks.'

'No. He got that injury before he went in the water.'

He said sharply, 'Nonsense, you can't tell that.'

'No. But he didn't go swimming and get drowned if that's what you think.'

'Why not? It's the most logical explanation.'

'There's nothing logical about it at all. Stuart never went swimming. He couldn't swim.'

Clive was assailed by a sense of unreality. He stared out across the sea to King's Rock, and thought of the man in his mid-forties who, except for a few years in World War II had lived all his life by the sea. He remembered seeing Stuart King fishing from a dinghy on the bay, manipulating a small sailing boat at Comedene further along the coast; puttering back and forth between Port King and King's Rock in his expensive little motor launch; talking knowledgably about his string of small boat-building yards from here to Penzance.

'Don't be ridiculous,' he said. 'He's wearing swimming shorts.'

'What else do you wear on a day like this if you've got any sense? Stuart couldn't swim.'

'It's not possible.'

'It is and I'll tell you how. When he was a little boy he had rheumatic fever. He was an only and precious child and his mother never let him go in the water. And because of his illness he was never taught to swim at school either. By the time he was grown up I suppose he was ashamed. So rather than admit it, he never learnt. And hardly anybody knows.'

He said slowly, 'It seems incredible.'

'Oh I don't know. It was just one of those matters of human pride being carried too far.'

The coolness of the remark and the clarity of her young voice made him suddenly aware of her. She had been right to rebuff him an hour—a lifetime?—ago. She might be still a teenager—he couldn't quite remember—but she was no longer a child. Already she spoke with the voice of authority, decisive, almost abrasive. Clare's voice was soft—slightly breathless; a soothing sound that he suddenly longed achingly to hear.

'Are you going to be sick?' asked the voice of authority surprisingly.

He shook his head. 'No.' He was silent for a moment. 'I suppose he must have fallen while he was fishing.'

Penny lifted her head from her knees and looked out over the sparkling water.

'I'd like to think so,' she said.

For a moment the sky seemed to cloud over and the sea roared in his ears. He turned his head to say something sharp to her; anything to ease the tension her words had created in him. But at that moment there was the sound of voices from the combe behind them, and the ringing of heels on the small jetty.

Clive got slowly to his feet and followed Penny who had already begun to move towards the oncoming figures. It was *their* business now he thought with infinite relief. If Penny had any more startling remarks to make, she could make them to the police.

.    .    .    .    .

Six hours later the household at King's View was preparing itself for bed, if not for sleep.

Stuart King's body had been removed to the nearest mortuary. The police, impassive, had taken statements, left a man on duty at Port King and gone away. A stunned Blanes had been met at the station by Clive, consoled by Maria and taken to spend the night with his sister in the village. Michael, after several vain attempts to get in at local hotels, had been installed in what had once been the housekeeper's bedroom. A little food and rather more liquor than usual had been consumed by those who could stomach it. The telephone had at last stopped ringing.

Maria creamed her face and brushed her hair and wondered at the normality of her movements. Behind the first overwhelming shock she had begun to feel the beginning of a genuine grief. Stuart, a few years younger than herself, had been her closest neighbour ever since her husband had bought King's View fifteen years earlier. As Bill Greatly was away a good deal, and Stuart himself was unmarried, they had naturally enough been paired off at local dinner parties and thrown together at other social gatherings and from a casual acquaintance they had form-ed an equally casual friendship. There were still gaps in their knowledge of each other and neither had looked for greater intimacy, but liking, respect, and even affection there had been. And now Stuart was dead—had died alone and unpleasantly while she had gone unknowingly about her normal, pleasant, daily routine.

She got up from her dressing table and went to the window for one more look at the beautiful cruel sea beyond the cliff edge. She stepped on to the balcony that fronted the house and looked out on a night that was perfect: unusually warm, deepest blue, deceptively peaceful.

On her right at the end of the house was Clare's room, a chink of light showing through rose-scattered curtains drawn against the night. At the opposite end was Clive's room. His curtains were undrawn and she could see the come and go of his cigarette end against the darkened window.

Obviously he too was contemplating the sea—the sea which he normally loved and which tonight can have been giving him very little pleasure.

What would today have been like without him?

She herself was by no means given to hysteria; Penny was cool-headed both by nature and training; Clare more volatile than either of them had been brought up to control her emotions. But how calm, how cool, how controlled would they have been if one of them had made that horrible discovery in the water?

As it was, they had taken their cue from Clive. And, it seemed to Maria, that from the beginning he had slipped into a position of power like a well-maintained machine programmed to behave perfectly through a trial of strength. Clive had dealt with the formalities, with the police, with the press. With John Tredger who was Stuart's solicitor and who, Maria noticed, had deferred willingly to the younger man, he decided on the list of people who must be informed at once of Stuart's death. And done much of the informing.

He had been gentle with the women, kind with Blanes, exacting with officials, firm with the curious, tactful with the press. Only once had he faltered and that had been when she, Maria, had asked him point-blank why Stuart's death could not be considered a straightforward case of drowning. He had turned suddenly and walked from the room leaving it to Penny to explain Stuart's injuries in the cool, impersonal tones of a medical student.

It was easier to remember then that he too was suffering shock and grief and that probably his machine-like efficiency was in itself a sort of armour against the reality of a friend's dead face in the peaceful water.

Maria did not know, and had no wish to inquire, how far the relationship between Clare and Clive had gone. But tonight, against all the rules of motherhood, contrary to all the beliefs in which she had been brought up, she found herself hoping that when the household was quiet, Clare would leave her room and go along the old creaking passage to join him.

.      .      .      .      .

Afterwards no one found it possible to say at what stage of the next day's proceedings it became clear that the police were not treating Stuart's death as accidental.

22

The police surgeon's report was presumably what clinched it in the minds of the police themselves but there was no perceptible change in the questions, only a sort of hardening of the concentration with which they asked them.

They were at their hardest and most concentrated with Clive but that, in the circumstances was understandable. What Maria didn't understand, as she met Clive in the flagged passage to the kitchen, was why he should look so grim. The interview had clearly been an ordeal.

'Maria, I want to talk to you. Quickly, before the Superintendent calls you in.'

'There's no one in the kitchen.' Bewildered she led him into the wide beautiful room. 'Who's with them now?'

'Penny. But they may not be long with her. I have to tell you something.'

She swallowed her fear and tried to be normal. 'Shall I make some coffee while you tell me?'

'All right. Yes, thanks.'

He sat down at the table while she occupied her hands with pots and pans, her brain racing.

'Where is Clare?' he asked suddenly. 'I haven't seen her this morning.'

'I don't know,' she answered truthfully. 'I thought she was with you till the Superintendent came.'

'No,' he said bleakly.

She was silent. She believed reluctantly that she knew where Clare was. Last evening she had gone with Michael, while he searched the district for a hotel room. And she had breakfasted with Michael that morning before Clive put in an appearance. Was she with him now? And if so, was it better to men-

23

tion it casually or to leave the words unspoken?

She was saved the decision. Clive changed the subject.

'Maria, don't be surprised if they ask you some rather strange questions. I think—I'm rather afraid —that they think it was suicide.'

'Suicide!' She turned to face him, wide-eyed. 'Oh no! Not Stuart.'

'Look, love, *I* don't know. But that's where their questions seem to be leading. And I thought you'd rather know.'

'But it's so unlikely. What made them think it?'

'They think he may have gone into the water from King's Rock. And they know now that he couldn't swim.'

'He could have fallen in.'

'How?'

'When he was fishing.'

'Penny says his fishing platform on the island is as safe as houses.'

'If the tide were low he might have gone down to the rocks.'

'He might.'

'But they don't think so?'

'His rods were apparently untouched.'

'I see.' She put a cup of coffee in front of him. 'Still, I don't believe it.'

'No? Maria, did he have any worries?'

.    .    .    .    .

'Did he have any worries that you know of?' The Superintendent repeated Clive's words.

Maria shook her head. 'None that I know of.'

24

'Financially he was all right?'

She shrugged her shoulders. 'I wouldn't know. I suppose Stuart wasn't rich compared with what his family had been in the past. But by ordinary standards he was more than comfortable.'

'His business all right?'

'I doubt if he'd have told me if it wasn't. But I think he'd have got rid of it before he let it bankrupt him.'

The Superintendent nodded. He was a taciturn man but not unsympathetic. He was the right man for the job because he was both local and in tune with the people in the case. He could believe that no King of King's Rock would fall into bankruptcy. About other things he was not so sure.

'What about women?' he asked abruptly.

'What about them?' She had always regretted that Stuart hadn't married because she thought his life a lonely one, and she had assumed there had been— and possibly still were—women for whom he had had more than a liking. But she knew none of them. He had often been away for short periods and she had thought there might be a woman, as well as business, involved. But she had no evidence of it.

She shook her head. 'I just don't know.'

It seemed to her that there was an ominous silence, which she could not break. Useless to say 'there weren't any young men either' because they both knew that this weekend there *had* been a young man, as handsome a young man as anyone could ever hope to meet.

Despondently she rejoined Clive who had taken his coffee out on the lawn and had been joined by Clare and Michael.

25

'They want you now,' she said to Michael, feeling treacherous.

'Well, goodness knows what they think Michael can tell them,' said Clare indignantly. 'They know Stuart had been in the water several hours and Michael didn't arrive till just before he was found.'

Michael was very pale but he managed to smile. 'There are other things they'll want to know,' he pointed out. 'When I last heard from him, how well I knew him, and so on.' He got to his feet. 'And very fishy it's all going to sound,' he said resignedly, and went off in the direction of the house.

'God knows,' said Clive, and closed his eyes.

'God knows what?' asked Clare.

'God knows the answer to all the questions Maria is asking in her mind.'

'The police will find out,' said Clare. 'And it was an accident. It must have been.' She touched his hand. 'Don't be so morbid.'

He opened his eyes and smiled at her, but he did not speak.

'Where's Penny?' asked Maria suddenly.

'Gone swimming,' said Clive and closed his eyes again.

There was a long silence.

'How could she?' said Clare at last. 'How could she?' For the first time her voice broke and her mouth quivered.

Clive sat up in his chair and pulled her into his arms.

'Don't, sweetie, don't. If you cry, so will Maria and I just won't be able to bear it.'

Her arms went round his neck and they clung together for a moment, his face buried in her hair, hers

26

in his shoulder. Maria waited, the tears pricking her own eyes, and stared over the glorious green of the grass to the glittering sea and the perfect sky.

'Clare, would you like to go away? Maria too if you like. We need only stay here another twenty-four hours I should think. Would you like to?'

Clare disentangled herself, composed again. 'Where would we go, it's difficult to get in anywhere at this time of the year.'

'Oh I don't know. Anywhere. Abroad perhaps. We'd find something.'

'What do you think, Mother?'

'I can't,' said Maria. 'Not yet. I think I must stay and help Blanes. And there's Penny. Four of us is too many. But you go. It's a good idea.'

'Shall we?'

It struck Maria that Clive was the more anxious to get away. Clare was hesitating.

'Let's wait a day or two to see how we feel. I don't think it's fair to leave Mum. Father won't be home for weeks.'

'Here's Penny.' Maria watched her approach much as she had watched her yesterday. She had obviously come straight from the water, her hair was still wet, her swimsuit clung to her. Susie romped beside her flinging a spray of water with every leap.

Penny threw herself down on the grass.

For a moment no one spoke. Then she said, 'Go on in, the water's fine.'

'I don't know how you could.' Clare spoke very low, not critically but bewildered.

Hugging her knees and staring at the horizon Penny said, 'It's the same sea, you know, the same beach, as it has always been. Men have been drowned and washed up here before. Men have been clubbed to death'—Clive made an involuntary movement and she turned her head towards him—'Smugglers not so long ago. Or they were shot and wounded and died in the coves. There is no difference between a swim today and a swim yesterday or a swim in a week's time.'

'There is to me.' Clare turned her head away.

'But you will one day. So why not now? Get it over.'

'Surgery rather than a lingering illness,' Clive remarked mockingly.

'Yes if you like. Don't tell me *you're* jibbing.'

'You weren't the one to find him,' said Clare.

'No, but I might have been. And so might you. You swam yesterday at low tide and I when it was just on the turn. We were lucky. But the worst is over now.'

'She's right, of course,' said Clive reluctantly. 'We can't stay forever on the cliffs. I *should* go.'

'Some other time,' said Maria.

'You don't agree with me?' asked Penny. It was a genuine question. Penny for all her assurance and young arrogance was always ready to listen to her aunt.

'I think you're a very tough young woman,' said Maria but she softened the words with a smile and met Penny's eyes.

'Penny regards that as a compliment,' said Clare grinning.

'Not any more,' said Penny with a sigh. 'I know I used to. But Maria means that I can do my own thing only I mustn't force it on other people.'

Maria nodded. 'That's about it.'

'I always shall,' said Penny despondently. 'I always shall.'

'Oh no,' said Clive kindly, 'you'll grow up one day, I expect.'

Maria felt a surge of thankfulness. This pleasant exchange of insults was a normal part of their usual conversation. For the first time since yesterday afternoon she felt a slight relaxing of the tension. And Penny did it, she admitted to herself honestly. Penny's the one who grasps the nettle danger.

'Michael's a long time,' said Clare suddenly.

'Is he with the Superintendent?' Penny asked. 'He's on the wrong track *there.*'

'Penny!' Maria hardly ever spoke sharply to her niece, though Penny, in the absence of her parents abroad, had spent many a school holiday at King's View. 'Don't say things like that!'

'Like what? I only meant *cherchez la femme,*' said Penny. She sounded—for Penny—quite humble.

'What *femme?*' Clive who had appeared to be asleep suddenly shot her a suspicious look.

'I don't know. Here's Michael.'

By tacit consent they were silent as Michael approached.

He said with a laudable effort at calm, 'I'm sorry, Clive, but now the Superintendent wants to see you again. And I am not to leave the district. I think at any moment now I'll be the man at the police station helping the police with their inquiries.'

'I thought they'd done with me.' Clive began to get slowly to his feet.

.     .     .     .     .

Superintendent Marshall stood up as Clive entered the room. 'I'd be very grateful for your help,' he said without preamble.

'What sort of help?' Clive took out his cigarettes. 'I've told you all I can.'

'We've checked your alibi,' said Marshall abruptly.

'And my credentials?'

'Yes.'

'I see.'

He was silent and the Superintendent moved uncomfortably. 'Shall we sit down?'

'All right. Will you smoke?' Clive offered his cigarettes without a trace of friendliness.

Going to be sticky, thought Marshall. Pity. Well, better press on.

'You are one of Mr. King's executors?'

'Yes.'

'Which implies that you knew him fairly well.'

'It may imply that but in fact I didn't. I think perhaps Stuart asked me because he didn't want anyone local to do it. That's all.'

'It gives you an entrance to his house?'

Clive stopped in the act of putting away his lighter. 'What does that mean?'

'If I send ham-fisted jacks to search the rooms the whole neighbourhood will be on to us in a minute.'

'Does that matter?'

'Yes, it does.' The Superintendent leant forward over the desk. 'Look, Mr. Richards, you know we have reason to believe this was neither accident nor suicide. King was killed and then put in the water.'

'No, I didn't know,' Clive said slowly. 'I suspected, but I didn't know. Since this morning I have been hoping it was suicide.'

'It wasn't.'

Clive spread his hands resignedly. 'Who would kill him? A harmless man.'

Unlike yourself, thought Marshall. Nothing harmless about you when the bit is between your teeth. Only just now it isn't.

'We've been over the house once,' he said. 'Last night, before the news was out. When you go there . . .'

'When . . .?'

'When you go there,' said the Superintendent firmly, 'will you look for anything unusual.'

'Such as?'

'Papers.'

'What sort of papers?'

Marshall was patient, but he was losing his cool. 'Well, for instance, we found this.' He picked up a cheque and handed it to Clive.

£2,000—to Michael Highstone. *Cherchez la femme*, Penny had said.

'What's that for?'

'I don't know.'

'What does *he* say? Highstone.'

'He says *he* doesn't know. Says he'd never seen it before.'

'Believe him?'

'Yes. It was in a locked bureau. We've no evidence that Highstone was ever in the house.'

'Blackmail?'

'Could be.'

'For what?'

'That's what we want to know.'

'I think Stuart liked women.'

'So do I,' said Marshall. 'So maybe Highstone was working with one. Or maybe he wasn't. What do you know about him?'

'Nothing.'

'Nor do we.'

'Checked his alibis?'

'They don't seem to check very well. Not like yours.'

'And his credentials?' asked Clive bitterly.

'They seem all right. He's a marine engineer, as he told us. He seems to have met King at a dinner and talked boat engines to him. King asked him down for a weekend. Highstone was rather surprised. But flattered. I suppose King was . . .'

'King,' said Clive. 'Yes, it *sounds* all right.'

King of King's Rock. What young man in the boat designing business wouldn't go for a weekend of quiet luxury if invited? And yet why, why should he be invited?

They both contemplated the thought for a moment, looking for flaws in the idea that this was to have been a perfectly normal social weekend shared by two perfectly normal men with common interests.

'Sorry,' said Clive abruptly. 'I don't think I can help you.'

The Superintendent turned his attention back to the man in front of him. He wanted his help; wanted it quite badly. But he did not relish the idea of demanding it from this tired-looking man who had come on a recuperative holiday only to drag the body of his friend from the sea. He had hoped that the mere suggestion of murder would influence

32

Clive Richards to offer his considerable knowledge and experience to the police but it seemed to have had the opposite effect. Well, in spite of what his pal at the Home Office had said, he wasn't going to push it. Not just now.

'If you don't feel you can,' he said, 'there is of course nothing to be done. The Home Secretary . . .'

'Damn the Home Secretary,' said Clive.

'He says you're on sick leave,' said Marshall austerely.

'Information supplied by the tenth secretary,' said Clive.

'Most of us,' said Marshall, 'don't rate the attention of even the twentieth secretary. I'm sorry to have bothered you.'

'Anyway it's not true,' said Clive rising and turning to go. 'I'm just on holiday. Good luck.'

'Thank you.'

Clive hesitated at the door, turned back and produced his disarming and entirely genuine smile. 'I'm sorry I can't help,' he said.

So am I, thought the Superintendent. So am I.

.     .     .     .     .

Clive was not accustomed to feeling either physically or mentally below par, and he did not approve of his present lethargy. Making a determined effort, he contacted John Tredger and set about his duties as one of the executors of Stuart King's estate. He went down to the village to talk to Blanes and make arrangements for looking after Port King. He had, he told himself, no intention of doing any police work.

33

*Cherchez la femme*, Penny had said. Why? What made her think that there had been a woman—or at least a woman of any importance—in Stuart's life.

Well, why shouldn't she think so? Penny was often at King's View, first during school holidays, then University vacations and long weekends. It was not surprising that she should know something about Stuart King.

He went back to King's View to find that Michael had gone off to try once again to find accommodation but had been told he could return to King's View if he failed.

'I honestly think he doesn't feel he should be here,' said Maria. She wondered worriedly why she was making excuses for him.

Clive shrugged, 'He'll be back. I doubt if there's an empty hotel room between here and the Scillies.'

The day was hotter even than yesterday. Clive longed to swim yet could neither persuade himself down to the cove nor indulge himself to the extent of driving along the coast to a more popular and less sinister beach. And Clare, though she had no horrifying picture of Stuart's dead face in front of her, was equally squeamish.

But as evening fell and the sun sank gloriously over the sea a telephone call from Blanes aroused Clive to action, albeit action of a dispirited kind. The Inspector's ham-fisted jacks had been over the house again, taken a few things away, photographed one or two apparently innocuous corners and gone away leaving one constable on duty. Blanes would be going back to the village to stay with his sister. Now, he asked what should he do about the Rolls in the garage, the motor dinghy in the inlet, the sailing boat in the boathouse, the silver, the unlocked desk drawers, the family portraits.

'Lock 'em up,' said Clive. 'You have the keys, don't you?'

'No, sir. I've been away for three weeks. Mr. King had all the keys.'

'Well, do you know where they are?'

'I expect I could find them, sir.'

'Then do.'

There was a long silence.

'I don't think I should, sir,' said Blanes at length. 'Some of the things are very valuable. Someone—someone like yourself, sir, should see they are all present and correct.'

Clive cursed himself for his tactlessness.

'Well, Blanes, I'll come if it'll make you happier.'

'Thank you, sir.' Blanes' voice sounded choked and Clive knew with a feeling of dread that this was not going to be easy.

'I'll be right down,' he said, and hung up.

He turned to find Clare standing beside him.

'You've got to go to Port King?' she asked.

He nodded.

'I'll come with you.'

'There's no need, love. I'll only be an hour or so.'

'Oh, let's do it together. And we'll give poor old Blanes a drink.'

It was much easier with Clare there. She knew the house almost as well as her own, she was on the best possible terms with Blanes; and she had been at Port King yesterday afternoon waiting for the police, so that for her the first sensitivity towards the masterless house was over.

The various keys were found, the Rolls firmly

locked; the paintings listed, the silver collected and put into a strong box for removal to the bank as soon as possible.

Blanes was instructed to caretake, to employ Mrs. Tresimmon whenever he needed to, to let Clive know of any correspondence that might arrive. Grieved and upset as he obviously was, Blanes was once again the perfect manservant, self-sufficient, all-encompassing, respectful without a touch of servility.

When all else was done he turned to Clare.

'There's a lot of food, Miss Greatly, arrived yesterday. Mr. King must have ordered it for the weekend. I wondered if your mother could use it.'

'You'll need some yourself, Blanes.'

'Not a whole turkey, Miss; or asparagus and all that pâté. I'd be obliged if you'd take some of it.'

'I'll go and see what there is.'

She went off towards the kitchen and Blanes helped Clive do some final locking up. Then he said awkwardly, 'I found something, sir, that I don't quite know what to do with.'

He felt in his pocket and produced a ring.

Clive looked at it with some foreboding. 'Where did you find that?'

'In Mr. King's bedroom, sir. It's a lady's ring.'

'Yes,' agreed Clive seriously. 'Even in these days there's no doubt about that.'

'And it's not Mr. King's mother's, sir. All her jewellery is in the bank.'

'No. This is fairly new. Why didn't you give it to the police?'

Blanes was silent a moment. Then he said, 'It seems such a shame, sir, it's probably quite unimportant. But it would Start Something. Can I give it to you, Mr. Richards?'

Clive sighed. 'Perhaps you'd better. It's only worth a few pounds but you'd better not conceal it. All right, Blanes, I'll deal with it.'

He slipped the ring into his own pocket and went to join Clare in the kitchen.

Clare had done a neat job of dividing the food into what Blanes would need, what could be given to Mrs. Tresimmon and what would best be consumed at King's View. Blanes offered to take it up to the house on his way to have his nightly drink at the Captain's Cabin.

Clive locked the french windows and stared out over the inlet to the beach and the sea beyond.

The evening was perfect. Gentle waves lapped against the empty sand at the tide's edge; the sun flooded the horizon with the afterglow, yet a heat haze still danced on the flat rocks. Dusk was beginning to touch the cliffs with black shadows. A lazy glamour shrouded the cove.

Without speaking they moved together across the terrace and towards the jetty and looked down at the boat tied up in the inlet.

'I'll leave it here. The—someone may be needing to go over to the Rock. But I'll lock the boathouse, the sailing boat is worth a packet.'

'Who inherits?' asked Clare suddenly.

'A cousin living in Spain. John Tredger's contacting him.' He looked around. 'I suppose the place may be sold.'

'And no more Kings of King's Rock.'

He smiled. 'It was not a very ancient dynasty, you know. A King bought it from the original owners after the Civil War. Before that it was just known as the Rock.'

'I wish,' said Clare, aggrievedly, 'that you wouldn't be so unromantic.'

'Oh, but I'm not.' He turned and pulled her into his arms. 'Believe me, I am not.'

For a moment there was only the soft to and fro of the sea to break the silence, as he kissed her long and hard. Then they moved into the shadows of the towering rocks and slid down on to the firm sand.

It seemed to Clive a lifetime since he had even touched her and the frustrations of the last few weeks had been crystallized into a fearful numbness ever since he had returned from his fateful swim, the day before. Now suddenly she was beside him and he could be restored to feeling.

This was how the cove could be restored too; back to its former peacefulness. Forget the nightmare of yesterday and make this the place where at long last he and Clare could be lovers.

At first it seemed to him that she responded willingly to his caressing hands. He was a skilful lover, by no means inexperienced, and normally he was a sensual rather than a demanding one.

But now he demanded. His hands, no longer caressing, were urgent and emphatic.

Here was the place; now was the moment. Here and now. Here, here, here—and now.

A seagull screamed high above them and she thrust him away with ferocity, almost with fear.

'No.'

'Oh God.' He fell back on the sand, staring up at the disappearing gull, the nightmare engulfing him again. This was not the place where he and Clare

38

were to be lovers; this was the place where Stuart—poor harmless Stuart—had been dragged from the sea.

'I'm sorry.' She was almost in tears. 'But I couldn't bear it. Not here. Let's go home.'

He closed his eyes for a moment, filled now with remorse. The monumental selfishness of his action horrified him. He had tried to use his beautiful Clare as if she were a bromide, a sleeping-draught, to cure him of what should be endured. He had wanted her purely for his own tranquillity and not because she wanted him or because he was overwhelmed with love. He had given no thought to her own feelings at his macabre choice of a trysting place. For macabre it had been.

He got up and pulled her gently to her feet, then kissed her without passion.

'Yes, we'll go home,' he said, and taking her hand led her up the zig-zag, averting his thoughts from the last time he had made this journey, deliberately trying to calm himself.

And he succeeded. By the time they reached the top of the cliff it was growing dark. In the distance the Long Point Lighthouse had begun its rhythmic flashing; far out at sea a lighted ship made a jewel on its dark setting. The lights were on at King's View but no curtains were drawn and the house looked normal and welcoming.

Very well, they would wait. No more scenes like that on the beach. As soon as the Stuart affair was settled they would fix a date for their wedding and go unfashionably chaste into marriage. He slid his arm companionably round her and was rewarded by a relaxing of her rigidity. All now would be well.

Susie heard their coming from a distance and bounded out of the dusk towards them, followed by Penny. They all walked together over the soft grass to the beckoning house.

At that moment Michael came out of the door and began to walk towards them, a tall dark figure illuminated only by the lights from the house. And as he moved, so did Clare, slipping from the gentle clasp of Clive's arm and making her way towards Michael as if to create some magic spell of her own. To Clive it was as if she had done far more than make a physical move away from him. She had removed herself irrevocably from his orbit into Michael's.

Yet the words Michael spoke were ordinary to the point of being sheepish.

'No luck,' he said. 'I'm just going to fetch my case and inflict myself on you once again.'

'Where did you try?' Without a backward glance Clare began to walk with him towards the side of the house. He slipped his arm through hers and apparently unconsciously she moved nearer to his side.

Clive sat down on the bench beside the front door and felt for his cigarettes. With them he pulled out from his pocket the ring that Blanes had given him. It lay in his hand, gleaming in the light from the hall.

'Know whose this is?' he asked Penny.

She barely needed to glance at it, so familiar it was to her.

'Sure,' she said. 'That's Clare's.'

.    .    .    .    .

Sunday morning had its particular quality of peace even here, where scattered houses and private beaches ensured a perpetual quiet. And this beautiful sun-washed day was no exception.

Penny emerged from the unbolted front door, took her customary adoring look at the shining semicircle of sea and set off, with Susie bounding round her, towards the village.

She looked stealthily up at the windows of King's View as she skirted the house. She *felt* stealthy, and a little mean, but in an unusually wakeful night she had made up her mind.

Superintendent Marshall who had been feeling slightly aggrieved at being, with his force, the only people astir, was slightly more aggrieved to find he wasn't. But he pulled out a chair and offered her a cup of coffee.

'Well, what can I do for you?'

'You can listen to what I have to say,' said Penny. 'And you may find the boot is on the other foot.'

He raised his eyebrows in surprise. He was not a man to underestimate his fellow human beings but it seemed that he probably had underestimated this very young redhead.

'I see,' he said. 'Well, what have you to say?'

'First,' said Penny going straight to the heart of the matter, 'I am quite sure that Stuart King was having an affair with someone—I don't know who —and I may be the only other person who knows about it. Secondly, I know that it is going to look very much as if that woman was my cousin Clare. And it wasn't.'

'Can you tell me how you know these things?'

41

'Yes I can, but you've got to bear with me—there are some things that need explaining.'

He was silent, ready to be unsurprised.

'Did you know,' said Penny, surprising him, 'that Stuart couldn't swim?'

'Yes. We discovered that.' So this was it—Stuart couldn't have been drowned, he would never have gone in the water. Marshall shifted uncomfortably.

'But my cousin was teaching him to swim.'

She had done it again. In his surprise he said, 'She didn't say so when I saw her yesterday.'

'No, because in her mind it wasn't relevant. Clare hadn't seen Stuart since Wednesday but she knew he'd *been* seen since then. So he didn't drown during a swimming lesson. Right?'

He said nothing.

She sighed. 'I know. Nothing's right till it's proved. But Clare is honest as the day. If she says something it's true. So I believe her, which gives me an advantage over you.'

This time he was really startled. His thoughts echoed Maria's of Friday afternoon—a force to be reckoned with, this one.

'I can see your point,' he said guardedly, 'but I still think she should have told me.'

'Of course she should. That's why I'm doing it now. You see Clare didn't even tell *me* she was teaching Stu to swim.'

'Why not?'

She stared for a moment into her coffee. 'She is a gentle girl,' she said at last, 'and she would not have wanted to hurt my feeiings—or Blanes'! It's all right, I know that's not clear, but I can explain. You see Clare is a goodish swimmer but nothing like as

42

good as I am. Blanes is a poor swimmer, he hardly ever goes in the water. The local people rarely can swim well, have you noticed?'

He nodded.

'Stuart was nervous of the water—not of being on it or near it but nervous to start swimming. Partly an inhibition left over from his mother's influence, partly a fear of making a fool of himself. So, of the very few people who knew he *needed* swimming lessons, Clare was the most likely person for him to turn to.'

'Not you?'

'No. He'd think I was too good for him, would expect too much of him. And Clare's a patient soul, whereas people think I am very impatient. As a matter of fact,' said Penny matter-of-factly, 'I am not.'

He hid a smile behind his coffee cup. He'd got a right one here but he was enjoying it.

'Anyway, that's it. About three weeks ago, when Blanes first went away, Clare began to give Stu swimming lessons.'

'You know this?'

'Yes. I could see them.'

'From King's View?'

She shot a look at him. 'Of course not. You can't see Port King or the Rock from the house, only from the cliff edge. But I was on King's Rock.'

'You were?'

'I had Stu's permission to go there whenever I wanted during the day. I love it, you see, I love the loneliness and the oldness, and the wildness. I sometimes go there to fish or to think or to read. And I studied there often, for hours on end.'

'How do you get there?'

'By my aunt's rowing boat, or by Stu's dinghy or I swim.'

'With your books on your head?'

'I used to leave some of them over there in the fishing store,' she said with dignity.

'O.K. So you saw them swimming from the beach. How did he get on?'

She gave him another penetrating look from under thick, unexpectedly black lashes. 'I couldn't really see. It's too far away. But I suspect not very fast.'

He nodded. 'So you know for certain those swimming lessons took place. That's what you're trying to establish.'

'Yes. I also know that Clare used Stu's bedroom to change in.'

This time he dropped his eyes and fiddled with a pen. But he waited.

'So did I sometimes. It's on the ground floor as you know and has french windows right out on to the sea terrace. But I usually wear my swimsuit all the time—like clothes, you know. Clare doesn't; she swims less, feels the cold more; wears a bikini which I don't, and is more modest than I am.'

'So Clare always came down to the beach dressed and changed in the house.'

'Yes.'

'And Stuart?'

'Like me,' she said briefly. 'He wore swimming shorts all the time and a sweater if it was chilly. When he went in the water he'd just chuck off his sweater.'

'So while your cousin was in the bedroom he was on the beach.'

44

'Yes. We've used his bedroom ever since we were kids. Clare was only ten when she came to live here, Stu was thirty. He was like an uncle. You use your uncle's bedroom to change in if he lets you.'

'Yes.' He nodded. 'You do. All right, you've established that. Your cousin was often in Mr. King's bedroom for perfectly respectable reasons. She isn't the woman in his life. Isn't that what you're trying to say?'

'Yes.'

'But you don't know who is?'

'No.'

'Then how do you know she exists?'

'Because one rather cold day I came back from the Rock and asked if I could borrow a sweater. Stu told me to go and get one. When I got it out it had a cleaner's tag on it and I went to the waste-paper basket to throw it away. And I saw a plastic bag that had had tights in it.'

'Not your cousin's?'

'She doesn't wear tights on the beach. Either bare legs or trousers. Besides she always wears chain-store tights. These were expensive.'

'That all?'

'No. I realized then that there were other signs— I saw powder, another thing Clare doesn't use —spilt on the dressing table. And a tissue with lipstick.' She looked up at him with a sudden flashing smile. 'I got rid of it all.'

'Why?' He was surprised into the question.

'Because Mrs Tresimmon *might* not have put two and two together but if she had, she'd have gossiped. Poor old Stu!'

Well, well he thought, this is the permissive

45

younger generation all right. Yet determined to protect her cousin. No, that's not true, she's not just protecting her; it's something else. She's *eliminating* her. With a flash of intuition, he asked, 'All right, what do you want me to do about it? Set about proving that there was no affair between your cousin and Stuart King and make sure Clive Richards knows I've proved it?'

She managed to surprise him again. Her eyes widened and her young fair-skinned face flared suddenly. A *blushing* permissive generation, he thought, and liked her even better.

'Put like that,' said Penny honestly, 'it does sound —well—impertinent. But yes—I suppose that's just what I do want. You see he—Clive—found a ring of Clare's, I think in Stuart's room.'

He sat back in his chair and lit a cigarette. 'This conversation is unofficial,' he said. 'You have perfect faith in your cousin. Don't you think Mr. Richards has too?'

'Normally, yes. But I don't think at the moment he's quite normal.'

'Still in a state of shock?'

'Yes, but more than that. He's been ill. And he had an accident.'

'What sort of an accident.'

'He hurt his foot quite badly.'

'How?'

'I don't know. And something went wrong with a job he was doing.'

'What sort of job?'

'I don't know,' she said. 'I don't see much of him.'

'Does your cousin?'

'See much of him? Not as much as she'd like.'

'Has there been a rift?'

'Well she was a bit upset because he wouldn't let her go to see him when he was ill.'

'Why wouldn't he?'

She shrugged. 'Pride, I suspect. Pride is something I'm suspicious of.'

'Why?'

'It leads people into deep waters. Oh . . .' she stopped and took a deep breath. 'Oh, what an awful thing to say.'

'But very true. You mean,' he said leading her gently back, 'that Mr. Richards didn't want your cousin to see him when he wasn't at his best.'

'Yes. I think so.'

'He'll have to when they're married.'

'I know, that's what's so silly.' She paused a moment. 'I think it's pretty silly anyway. A good old row I can understand but coolnesses baffle me.'

'Was there any other reason for it—the coolness I mean?'

She hesitated before answering, then lifted her eyes to his and gave him a long appraising look.

'I think she might have tried to persuade him to give up his job.'

'I see. Well, that's quite a thing to ask a man. I take it he refused.'

'I'm sure he did,' she said dismissively.

He would not be dismissed.

'Why did Miss Greatly want him to give up his job?'

'It takes him away a lot.'

'Couldn't she go too once they are married?'

'No.'

'What sort of job is it then?'

47

'I don't know,' she said. 'He's a civil servant. But I imagine he could go to another branch.'

'But he likes the job he has.'

She let out a small impatient sigh. 'I've never asked him.'

'Did he get hurt on his job? Is that why Miss Greatly doesn't like it?'

'I don't know.'

'What do you think?'

'If he got hurt on his job and if there's a chance of his getting hurt again of *course* she doesn't like it.'

'Yes,' he agreed sitting back. 'That's logical.'

'End of interrogation?'

'Not quite. Even supposing you're right about this—er—rift, do you think Mr. Richards should jump to conclusions about Miss Greatly and Mr. King?'

'No!' she said vehemently. 'He *shouldn't*. Clare shouldn't have not told you about the swimming. Someone shouldn't have hit Stuart on the head and thrown him in the sea. People *do* things they shouldn't.'

'Miss Keats,' he said, sitting up again, '*please* don't go round saying that. Anyway what makes you think it?'

'I saw him,' she said briefly. 'He got hit on the head first, drowned afterwards.'

'I forgot. You're a doctor.'

'You know quite well I'm not,' she said evenly. 'And if the police surgeon says I'm wrong, I'm wrong. But I don't think I am.'

He let that go.

'All right,' he said. 'This is still unofficial but I'll do what you want. I'll make sure Mr. Richards is

48

aware of your cousin's non-involvement in the case. All right?'

'It's not quite what I said,' she answered, getting to her feet. 'But it'll do.'

'By the way, what did he do with the ring? Give it back to Miss Greatly?'

'I don't know,' she said. 'You see it wasn't until —well—when I said it was Clare's ring I realised what I'd done. If I'd thought quickly enough I'd have offered to give it back to Clare and brought the whole thing out in the open. But I didn't.'

'Will he give it back to her, do you think?'

'I don't know.' She looked at him with a faint smile. 'I interfere quite a lot but not as much as that.' She went to the door and whistled up a recumbent Susie.

'You won't forget, will you,' she said, 'that I've given you some information?'

He smiled. 'No, I won't,' he promised but when he turned back into the little police station the telephone was ringing. The evidence was beginning to come in.

.     .     .     .     .

Penny got back to King's View in time for breakfast and was still brooding over her final cup of tea when Clare announced her intention of going down to Port King.

'I think I left my agate ring,' she said.

Penny, while burying herself in her cup was nevertheless conscious that the hitherto silent Clive had made an inquiring noise.

'I think,' said Clare, reaching for the butter, 'that

49

I must have left it in Stu's bedroom last time I changed in there.'

'Very sinister,' said Michael, passing her the marmalade. 'Have you a story ready?'

She looked up at him and smiled. 'As good a story as yours.'

'Well, love,' he said suddenly sombre, 'if I've got to be in trouble, I'd like to be in it with you.'

Penny put her cup down sharply. 'Clive has your ring, Clare,' she said crisply.

In the sudden silence they all looked at Clive, who drew the ring out of his pocket and put it on the table.

'Blanes gave it to me yesterday,' he said. 'Sorry, Clare.'

She slipped it on to her finger, and nodded her thanks.

Michael got to his feet. 'Well, now that you've been cleared, perhaps you'd like to come with me,' he said to Clare.

She laughed. 'Where to?'

'To try to find a room for me!'

'I'll come with you,' she said, getting up from the table, 'but I hope we don't find one.' She moved to the door and stopped. 'Coming, Clive?'

He shook his head. 'I've got to go down to Port King.'

'Lunch at 1.30,' said Maria suddenly emerging from her newspaper, 'and I've asked a few people for drinks.'

They looked at her sombrely.

'We've got to get the gossiping over some time,' she said. 'Let it be quickly.'

.    .    .    .    .

50

The people for drinks were the ones who had been there on Friday, plus Rowena's husband. George Carter was one of those businessmen who always managed to give the impression that they are only staying a moment because they have somewhere more important to go. Today this impression was stronger than ever. He had, he said, arrived at Merrynmouth late last night and was leaving again first thing next mornning. Meanwhile he had come to offer condolences to Stuart King's more intimate acquaintances.

Rowena looked pale and dispirited. Not even her hair and make-up were as perfect as usual. It occurred to Maria that she had been badly and genuinely shocked by Stuart's death and would have preferred her husband not to discuss it.

Maria herself was feeling put out. Whereas Penny and Clive had presented themselves in plenty of time to help carry the drinks out on to the lawn, Clare and Michael had not yet arrived. When they did come it was hideously reminiscent of the day before yesterday as they crossed the grass towards the others. And yet there was a difference. Before they had come together but separately, today they came as a pair. They said nothing, they did nothing to suggest intimacy. It simply existed.

Maria watching Clive pour drinks for everyone was conscious of a tension she could not ease. She took refuge in the inevitable gossip about Stuart.

It was, however, gossip of a highly civilized nature. They had all been fond of Stuart to some degree or another and the shock of his death had hardly begun to penetrate, let alone to wear off. Also, since John Tredger had been his solicitor there

51

was a certain reluctance to do any more than skim the surface. There would, John told them, be an inquest; he had no information beyond that. The cousin in Spain was coming to England as soon as he could get away from family and business ties. 'We shall have to get together tomorrow,' he said to Clive, and added after a moment, 'if you're feeling up to it.'

Penny twisted her head slightly and took a look at Clive over the rim of her glass. He *does* look rotten, she thought, but he won't like it referred to. And there popped unbidden into her mind a thought that was to affect all their lives within the next few days. *He's not prepared to admit he's lost his grip. Which means that he hasn't.*

'I'll come down to your office tomorrow,' said Clive to John Tredger. 'What time?'

'That's it. Get it over with,' George encouraged him. 'It's got to be done and the sooner the better. When's the funeral?'

There was a slight pause while they all deferred to each other. Then John said, 'Tuesday, I hope. After the inquest.'

'Oh! Oh I'm sorry about that.' George sounded genuinely regretful. 'I'd have liked to come and pay my respects, but I can't stay till Tuesday. Rowena will come though.'

'Oh no,' Rowena sounded frightened. 'I couldn't. I've never been to a funeral.'

'But you'll go to this one,' he insisted. 'It's not as if you're a member of the family.'

'They're so macabre,' she protested. 'I don't believe in them.'

'If you've never been to one you can't judge,' he said genially. 'You'll represent me.'

'You can come with me, Rowena,' said Maria, 'if George feels you should go.'

'George feels she should go,' said George. 'And George feels we should go home now, I've work to do this afternoon.'

Rowena swallowed the rest of her drink and got up, without argument. Maria, feeling sorry for her, promised to let her have details of time and place of the funeral as soon as possible.

The others began to move too, rather subduedly agreeing to meet either at the inquest or at the funeral.

Maria collected up the glasses with a heavy heart. The long-awaited time when they would all be on holiday together had gone sour. The sun blazed away as it had not done for years but it blazed on a saddened and somehow disjointed group.

.　　.　　.　　.　　.

It was still blazing when the police arrived, plain-clothed, in a small unpretentious car, and asked Michael to accompany them to the police station. There were they said, very politely, a number of questions he might be able to answer, details on which he could probably help them.

White to the lips he managed to smile. 'What did I tell you?' he said. 'The man at the police station who is helping the police.'

He rose gracefully to his feet. 'Shall I need my suitcase?'

53

'It might take some time, sir,' said the sergeant. 'I'll come with you to get it.'

He flinched. 'Yes, of course.' He turned to Clive. 'I wonder if you'd mind ringing my landlady . . .'

'We'll do that, sir,' said the sergeant. 'And your office.'

'There'll be no need for that,' he said with sudden spirit, 'I've already telephoned my boss to say I'd like to stay here for the inquest and the funeral.'

'Sergeant,' Maria felt compelled to say something. 'Is there anything we *can* do? I'm sure we should like to help Mr. Highstone.'

'The Superintendent will let you know, madam, if there is. Ready, sir?'

'As ready as I ever will be,' said Michael. 'Goodbye, Clare.'

She was suddenly on her feet and her arms were round him. 'It'll be all right. I know it'll be all right.'

He returned her kiss before detaching himself gently. 'Yes, of course. Thank you.'

Without another word he turned and walked with the sergeant across the glittering grass, followed by Maria.

Clare, Penny and Clive were left alone. Clare threw her arm across her eyes and let the tears slide down over her beautiful cheekbones. Penny sat mechanically ruffling Susie's curly stomach, her brilliant head bent to hide her own eyes. And Clive sat like a stone, his arms behind his head, his face expressionless, his eyes empty.

.    .    .    .    .

There was a limit to what Clive could do as executor because the police needed access to many of Stuart's private papers. But there were certain things that could be done and, for as long as possible during the hours that followed, Clive did them.

An open verdict was declared at the inquest and Clive guessed that Superintendent Marshall was not pleased. But except for one or two brief formal exchanges he had not talked to the Superintendent at all. He had given evidence of finding Stuart's body, an ordeal that seemed to him no worse than the many other ordeals he had survived recently.

He was not sure, however, how many more he could survive and he felt quite positive that there would be others if he continued to stay here. But there had been no more talk of going away and he knew Clare would not want to go while Michael was still under suspicion. Not that he had discussed it with her. There had been no conversation between them. Neither of them had mentioned what he now almost regarded as an attempt to rape her. They had never discussed Michael. He did not even know whether she was aware that for the length of one awful night he had suspected her of an affair with Stuart. Except on a purely social level, all communication between them had ceased.

But this could not last; in the end there must be a showdown of some kind. He felt no inclination to precipitate it; he merely continued to regard the present state of affairs as a feat of endurance. And feats of endurance were something to which his life had made him accustomed.

Now as he entered Stuart's study he became aware

of somone outside on the terrace and crossed to the window to see who it was.

Sitting in her familiar position, legs drawn up and her cheek on her knees, was Penny. And he knew she had come to find him. He went to join her.

'You looking for me?'

'Yes.' She looked round at him as he came towards her. 'How mean you are to keep coming here without Clare.'

He was breathless with astonishment.

'Clare wouldn't want to come here.'

'Have you asked her?'

'No.' Involuntarily his eyes turned towards the strip of silvery sand under the rocky cliff. 'But I'm afraid I know without asking.'

'She's very unhappy,' said Penny.

'My dear girl,' he said taking out his cigarettes, 'so am I. But I really don't see what it has to do with you.'

'You should be helping Michael.' The words seemed to burst from her as if she had been bottling them up and could no longer control them.

He stared at her in amazement. 'I should? What can *I* do?'

'You could be doing a bit of detective work.'

He made a business of lighting his cigarette. 'Who do you think I am? Lord Peter Wimsey?'

'I know who you are,' she retorted.

'A civil servant.'

'Yes,' she agreed. 'A very special civil servant— the one who was mentioned in the *Sunday Times*. "A brilliant operator even in a department renowned for its achievements." '

56

'Good Lord!' he said, not very flatteringly, 'fancy *you* reading that!'

'*You* did.'

He grinned. 'Well yes, the temptation was too great. But how did you know—I mean my name was never mentioned.'

'No, but you had just come home from a mission and you had been sent up to Harrogate for special conferences. It said all that. All it left out was your name.'

There was another silence.

'All right, Penny,' he said at length. 'I'm in a security job, sometimes on secret work, sometimes not. I can tell you that much. But that doesn't make me James Bond and I'm not proposing to teach the police their job.'

'But you could help them,' she insisted. 'Surely you could help them.'

'Why should I?' he asked. 'It seems to me I'm the last person who should be expected to get Michael Highstone off the hook.'

She did not answer him immediately and he looked up and caught the look in her dark brown eyes. For the first time he became aware that there might be an element of hero-worship in her feelings towards a man who was officially regarded as brilliant in a mysterious and dangerous job. He did not look upon his work as mysterious but much of what he did was classified as secret so, of course, to other people it *was* mysterious. Dangerous it had often proved to be but since the dangers went unseen to the general public it had never occurred to him that they gave him glamour. Penny knew as well as Clare did that this recent accident had been no ordinary one. Both girls had learnt not to ask questions but that did not mean they weren't curious.

Now he caught a glimpse of himself as Penny saw him—an invincible figure who had suddenly shown his feet of clay. No, worse, he had shown a streak of utter meanness. She did not like the new image and now that he thought about it, neither did he. What was worse, he realised with a wry inward smile, he did not like the idea of losing the hero-worship in one sudden blow. He would have preferred her to grow out of it gradually as she gained maturity. Or, he wondered, self-critically, did he want to preserve it?

She said in a subdued voice, 'But that's the very reason why you should.'

'What?' He had travelled so far in his thoughts that he had lost the thread of hers.

'If she has really fallen in love with him, she'll be so desperately miserable. Surely you'll want to help her. Even if she hasn't—if it's only a passing thing and she's just sorry for him—the sooner he's off the hook the better. You can't leave him hanging there.'

'Can't I?' He sighed. 'Penny, you had better face facts; I am not Sir Galahad either. I'm flaming well jealous of Michael Highstone, who is younger, taller and better-looking than myself. But you are, of course, perfectly right and I will see if there is anything that can be done for him.'

She said, turning her head away from him and gazing out at the Rock. 'There's one thing you may not know.'

'I really can't understand why you're asking my help. You seem to be a natural sleuth.'

'I talk to the villagers,' she said.

'Yes,' he agreed heartily. 'We know that.'

'Well, the rumour is that one reason why the police are suspicious of Michael is that he arrived here on Friday earlier than he said he did.'

He absorbed that for a moment. 'It figures,' he said at length. 'He was seen, I suppose?'

'Yes, wandering round the house.'

'That is bad, Pen. But perhaps he can explain why.'

'Perhaps he can. But if he *hasn't*—well I have a theory.'

'I might have known.'

'Stop fooling and listen to me. You have to try and understand this and you won't find it easy.'

His attention was caught by her earnestness. 'All right, I'm in my trying-to-understand mood. Go on.'

'I think when he got here and found no one in the house he was horribly embarrassed.'

'Well, it was embarrassing.'

'Yes, but I mean quite seriously so. He really didn't know what to do. He might have thought Stu was one of those people who hurl invitations about, never meaning them at all. He might have wondered if he'd boobed himself about the date or the time or even the place. And he was too shy to do anything about it.'

'Shy! Oh, come off it, Pen, he's a grown man and a very attractive and self-assured one . . .'

'Attractive, not self-assured.' She looked him up and down with a sudden flicker of anger. '*You* can't understand it because you *are* self-assured, but look at you—you've got the lot haven't you?'

59

'Oh yes,' he agreed. 'Beauty, brains, charm, lovable ways, everything but my girl.'

'Your looks are good enough,' she said briefly, 'but I meant the other things—education, background, family—even money, haven't you?'

'A little.'

He was looking at her in some surprise. He had not suspected the gregarious Penny of such sensitivity. She turned away again, resting her head on her knees. 'Michael hasn't,' she said. 'He's out of his depth with characters like Stuart King. He'd have been all right if Stu had been there and welcomed him and made him feel part of the scene. As it was his confidence went and he didn't know what to do next.'

'So he did nothing.'

'I imagine. Just wandered about hoping Stu would turn up, till finally he went back to the house and met Clare—and then he couldn't bring himself to tell anyone he'd been hanging around loose for two or three hours.' She paused. 'Well, how does that grab you?'

He sighed and rose to his feet. 'It grabs me,' he said. 'You may be wrong but you could be right. Sir Galahad is on his horse again.'

'*Cherchez la femme,*' said Penny.

'For God's sake stop using that awful cliché. I can't imagine what sort of books you read.' He walked away and then turned back to her. 'There's just one thing you should remember. If I probe I may turn up things *against* Michael, rather than for him.'

'Let's have the truth,' said Penny.

. . . . . . .

To Clive's surprise Superintendent Marshall welcomed him.

'I hope you've changed your mind,' he said, pulling forward a chair.

'Yes, I have. I don't know what I can do, but if you can use me, do.'

'You know the local people and they'll talk to you. I want to know if any of them had ever met or heard of Michael Highstone.'

'Um.' Clive pondered a moment. 'What do you know about him?'

'Clever. Highly valued in his job. Poor but respectable family. Father dead. Mother living with *her* mother in the Channel Islands. Won scholarship and grants, took a good degree, been with the same firm ever since. Lives in a small furnished flat in Rochester with a landlady who does for him.'

'Mm.' Clive did not meet the Superintendent's eye. 'Sounds good. Girl friends?'

'We're checking. No one obvious. No obvious men friends either. Just acquaintances.'

Clive looked up. 'Sounds even better. What have you got him for?'

'Questioning.' said the Superintendent.

Clive smiled. 'Yes, all right. Why?'

'Because of the cheque, because he doesn't seem to be able to explain why he's here. Because he lied. He said he arrived at 4.30 on Friday. We've found people who saw him at 2.15.'

'Asked him why?'

'Yes. Said he must have made a mistake.'

'You don't believe him?'

'No.'

'I suppose I can't talk to him?'

'Yes,' said the Superintendent surprisingly. 'You can. Oh, and there's something else you can do for me.'

'Yes?'

'We'd like to fingerprint all the people we know have been in King's house, especially the bedroom. Which means asking Mrs. Greatly and Miss Greatly and Miss Keats, all of whom occasionally used his bedroom to change in when they went swimming.'

Clive nodded. 'You'd like me to soften the blow.'

'If you would.'

'I'm sure they'll understand.'

The Superintendent nodded. He felt a great relief that he had kept his promise to the little redhead. He only hoped it had been unnecessary.

. . . . .

Face to face with Michael, Clive had a curious feeling that it was he who was on trial. The young man looked pale and worried but his manners were still perfect. He greeted Clive with surprise and gratitude.

'You do realize, don't you,' said Clive without preamble, 'that you don't have to stay here? As long as you make yourself available to the police they won't detain you.'

'I have nowhere to go,' he answered simply. 'If they're going to keep wanting to talk to me I may as well be here. But I'm going to the funeral tomorrow.'

Clive nodded. 'What have you been able to tell the police?'

'Nothing.'

'Will you try to tell me what I want to know? I'd like to try and help you.'

'Why?' The question was so direct that Clive was thrown momentarily off his balance. Why indeed? But it gave him a moment to think and almost at once he saw his opportunity.

'Because I think you've had a raw deal. You told one small social lie, about the time you arrived—a lie anyone might have told—and it's landed you here. A suspect, let's face it.'

He was accustomed to dissembling, and his own small social lie came easily to his lips, as if he had been rehearsed. As indeed he had, he thought grimly.

He had hit the right note. Michael smiled a little forlornly but at least he smiled.

'I didn't know what the hell to do or who to ask. I just hoped all the time that Stuart would turn up and all would be well. You see I wasn't even perfectly sure I'd got the arrangements right. I *thought* I had but when I found the house was empty I began to wonder if I'd confused the dates or time or something. And, of course, I hadn't brought his letter.'

'You're sure now that you were expected.'

'Yes. Whether it helps I don't know but Blanes says he was sure Stuart was expecting someone and Mrs. Tresimmon says she was told to prepare a bedroom. That part looks all right.'

'How did you get to know Stuart?'

'I didn't—really. I met him twice—once at our offices and then some weeks ago I happened to sit next to him at our firm's anniversary dinner. We got on well both times and he told me where he lived and I said it sounded beautiful and he said perhaps

I'd like to visit him. But I didn't take it seriously till a couple of weeks later he wrote and asked whether I could get some time off and come down here. Well, as it happened I was going on a series of engine tests so it was another fortnight before I was free but when it was over I would have some time off owing to me. So I said this weekend and he wrote back and said he'd expect me Friday afternoon as early as I liked. That was all. I really didn't know him.'

'But you wanted to come?'

'Yes. I liked him and . . .' He hesitated.

'And . . .'

'He was a good contact. He wasn't in the market for my particular speciality but he was interested in other aspects of my work. He buys—bought—a lot of boat engines.'

'What is your speciality?'

'An almost silent engine. Very expensive.'

'You mean no *put-put*?'

'Exactly that. Can you imagine it?'

'It's hard. Is there a market for it?'

'Yes, a small one. But Stuart was very honest about it. He was interested academically but his demand was for a servicable, hardworking small engine for pleasure boats. His own boat is an expensive one but the ones he builds are—well the everyday family holiday sort.'

'All right then,' said Clive suddenly. 'Why *did* he invite you?'

Michael went rigid with embarrassment. 'I don't know.'

'And why did he write you a cheque for £2,000?'

'I don't know.'

'Don't you think it funny?'

'I am not queer,' Michael said with sudden force. 'And I don't believe Stuart was either. I suppose the cheque was a bribe of some kind but I don't know what I was supposed to do to earn it. And I don't expect you to believe me.'

'What makes you think Stuart wasn't queer?'

'Nothing. That's it. Nothing indicated that he was. And I'd have said he liked women.'

'Did he talk about them?'

'No.'

'Then how do you know he liked them?'

'I don't. I just think he did.'

'You must have had a reason. He must have said something, implied something, given you some sort of hint.'

'Why must he?' Michael's calm was beginning to go. 'I don't get it. I...'

Clive leant across the table. 'Because, you ass, you would not have accepted his invitation if he hadn't. You say you aren't queer and I believe you. But when an unmarried man in his forties invites a good-looking man in his twenties for a weekend, you'd expect the warning lights to go up. You say they didn't. So he must have consciously or unconsciously, given himself clearance.'

There was a silence and then Michael let out a long sigh. 'Yes. I see. But I didn't think ...'

He paused and Clive waited.

'Yes. You're right. It was after that dinner. It was still only about ten o'clock when we broke up and I invited him to have a drink with me. But he looked at his watch and said he was sorry he had a date.

65

I assumed it was with a woman.' He thought for a moment. 'Doesn't help much, does it?'

'It might. It might not.' Clive sighed and pulled out his cigarettes. 'It's that damn cheque. Why would anyone write a huge cheque like that before he'd even made an offer? That's what's getting under Marshall's skin, and it's not surprising.'

．　　．　　．　　．　　．

Clive walked slowly back to King's View deep in thought, and glad to have something about which to think deeply. Michael's problem was at least taking precedence over his own troubles which now lurked depressingly in the back of his mind instead of in the front of it.

Soon he and Clare would have to heal their breach or widen it. Even if Michael were to go out of her life again in the next few days there would still be a breach.

Clive knew Clare well enough to be confident that she was not deliberately trying to make him jealous. Nor was she making a deliberate play for Michael. She was the most unflirtatious girl he had ever met and her faults were of the impulsive, not the calculating kind.

But she had turned to Michael with a kind of relief—an easing of tension, a lightening of mood that had been intensely hurtful—more hurtful than the actual turning away from himself.

Something had gone badly wrong in their relationship and it was almost certainly he who had caused it. Soon he would have to conduct a self-examination and find out what had gone wrong. But for the moment he would concentrate on who killed Stuart King.

Over lunch he reported some of his thoughts. Maria and Clare listened in a rather stunned silence, Penny with an air of abstraction as if the whole thing was too old hat to be interesting.

'So,' he concluded, 'even if she had nothing whatever to do with Stuart's death, it would be useful to know if this woman existed, just because it might help to prove Stuart wasn't being blackmailed because he was queer.'

'I've never heard such nonsense,' Clare said suddenly. 'Stu wasn't queer, neither is Michael. It's so obvious it's silly.'

'Prove it,' said Penny.

'I don't need to, I know.'

'Yes,' said Penny calmly, 'so do I. But we have to prove it.'

Clive turned to Maria. 'What do you think?'

'I think there was a woman,' said Maria slowly, 'but I don't know why I think it.' She smiled apologetically at Clive. 'Just intuition, I think.'

'And you, Clare, do you think there is?'

'Yes,' she said explosively.

'Why?'

'Just wishful thinking,' Penny answered for her.

Clare sighed. 'Perhaps, yes. I haven't any more reasons than Mum.'

'And Penny is sure there was one. But who was she, Pen?'

Penny went thoughtfully on with her lunch. 'She wasn't young. Probably about Stu's own age. And she was probably quite well off. And beautiful probably. And married.'

67

Maria put down her knife and fork and stared at her niece. 'Have you got someone in mind?'

Penny shook her head. 'No, but I know she wore expensive tights even on summer days on the beach. And used loose powder. Both older women things. Do you agree?'

Clare nodded and Maria glanced hopelessly at Clive who permitted himself a small half-smile.

'Also,' Penny went on, 'Stu wasn't a mixer, he stuck to his own type; so she was probably fortyish and fairly rich. Yes?'

Again Clare nodded.

'And why,' said Clive gently, 'was she married?'

'Because otherwise why not come out in the open? Stuart wasn't a secretive man and if he'd had an unmarried marriageable girl friend he'd have introduced her to his friends, taken her about. He'd have shown her off, not hidden her away.'

Maria agreed. 'If there *was* anyone, I think Penny's right. But, Clive, what good is this doing? Stuart's not very likely to have been killed by his girl friend.'

Clive looked at her despondently. 'No. But there's a chance of blackmail isn't there? The trouble is . . .' He stopped. The trouble was that if it was blackmail who was the blackmailer and why was there a cheque for £2,000 made out to Michael Highstone?

He said suddenly, surprising himself, 'I think I may go to London tomorrow after the funeral. I'll try and get back the next day.'

There was a moment's silence broken by Penny, 'What for?'

'I'd like to talk to Michael's boss.'

Clare put down her knife and fork and looked across at him, puzzled and a little frightened. He felt he knew why Victorian actors put their hands to their hearts to portray emotion, his own had started to pound uncomfortably, but the emotion, he knew, was a mixed one, neither sexual nor romantic, but born of resentment, jealousy and fear.

He put out his hand and covered hers. 'I'm trying to help, love,' he said.

She refused to meet his eyes and he knew that she was on the verge of tears. But somehow he felt a little easier; they were coming close to admitting what was between them. He had always found it easier to look a danger in the face than to pretend it wasn't there.

'Clive,' said Maria. 'This is not your business. Surely the police . . .'

'The police,' he interrupted her smoothly, 'have already talked to Michael's boss.'

'Then why should you? I'm not trying to be obstructive and I know you have helped the police before, but what can you do that they can't?'

Again there was an ominous silence. Penny's fork clicked on her plate. She seemed to be the only one with any appetite. When Clive spoke, it was gently, almost apologetically.

'Maria, the police have certain very good reasons for being suspicious of Michael. Naturally enough they are looking for facts that might bolster their suspicions, even prove them. I'm looking for facts to dispel them.'

Maria was horrfied. 'Do you mean . . .'

'I *don't* mean,' he said patiently, 'that the police twist facts; or that they find a likely-looking suspect

69

and then pin things on him. I only mean that they might overlook something in his favour while noticing something that is not. I want to know more about Michael.'

.    .    .    .    .

After lunch Clive went back to the village to talk to Superintendent Marshall. Maria watched him go with a feeling of acute depression. He looked like a man dragging himself to an ordeal.

'I wish,' she said, to her daughter, 'that you would persuade him not to go to London. He looks exhausted, he needs a few days' rest.'

Clare answered without catching her mother's eye. 'I don't see how any of us can rest just now,' she said.

Maria turned to Penny who was sitting in a deckchair, immersed in a text book. She flicked her aunt a look under the lashes that had so astonished Superintendent Marshall and said, 'He's still got something to give.' Then she returned to her book.

Maria was dismayed and somewhat chilled by what she felt to be callousness on the part of both girls. And she wondered why it was that the three younger people seemed banded together in the cause of an almost complete stranger: a man from outside their own group, who had lied to the police, behaved suspiciously and appeared—very reasonably—to be suspected of murder. For once she felt they had left her out.

.    .    .    .    .

'By all means see his boss,' said Superintendent Marshall. 'I can't hold him much longer for questioning though he's agreed to stay on a few days longer.'

'Is he, or isn't he under suspicion?' Clive asked the question directly, fairly sure he would get an indirect answer.

He did.

'King died some time in the early hours of Friday morning. That's as close as we can get because of the state of the body. Highstone *says* he left home early on Friday morning, had some lunch on his way and arrived here in the early afternoon, when he was seen in the village. But no one seems to have seen him set off.'

'And no one saw him on the way down?'

Marshall shrugged. 'He'd filled his car up on Wednesday night—the garage remembers that. He had enough petrol to get him down here. He filled up again in Merrynmouth. He ate lunch, he says, at the motel at Tormouth, but so far no-one there has identified him. Not surprising—big, crowded, self-service and most of the help is part-time. We're still checking.'

'You think he might have come down on Thursday night?'

'It looks as if he could have,' said the Superintendent cautiously. He paused, 'There's something else though.'

Clive waited. The sun poured through the windows of the little room, and danced dazzlingly on a glass vase into which someone had stuck a bunch of big-eyed daisies. From outside in the little street came the cheerful sound of voices of people bent

71

on pleasure—making their way to the quay, to the coves, to the car park at the edge of the village.

'We think it's likely,' the Superintendent went on, 'that Stuart was killed at King's Rock, not at his house.'

'Why?'

'Because if he'd been killed on the mainland his body would probably have been washed up earlier. if he was killed on the island it could have been caught up in the rocks and come in on the second tide.' He paused for a moment. 'What do you think?'

'For one reason and another,' said Clive slowly, 'I think you're probably right. But it poses a number of other questions.'

'Like who brought the boat back? Yes. Highstone's fingerprints are not on the boat. Or on the island. Or in the house. But he's a boating man. He could have got out there at night, wearing gloves. He *could* have.'

'But you don't think he did.'

'It would have had to be not only premeditated but pre-planned. It doesn't seem likely.'

'But you think he may know who did kill Stuart?'

'He may.'

'Do you think he was blackmailing him?'

The Superintendent shrugged. 'Cheques aren't made out direct to the blackmailer. But I want to know what that cheque was for. And Highstone *must* know that.'

Clive was silent. It did indeed seem likely.

.    .    .    .    .

The night was almost as hot as the day. Clive, gently opening the front door, wondered why he did not hear the soft inquiring growl with which Susie usually greeted unusual noises and happenings. Then he noticed that the door of the kitchen was open. Susie was not there.

So it was not altogether with surprise that as he reached the cliff edge he saw Penny coming towards him, a dark long-legged figure in a short beach coat.

'Clive?' she said so softly that he automatically answered her as softly.

'Did you hear it too?' She was beside him now, a well-disciplined Susie at her heels.

'Hear what?' He glanced down at her and saw that she had her swimsuit under the towelling coat. 'Penny, you weren't going swimming again?' he asked threateningly.

Two years ago when Clive had first come to King's View Penny had been discovered going for lone moonlight swims. Even the easy-going Maria had put her foot down about that. And even Penny a law unto herself, had been impressed.

Now she shook her head regretfully.

'No, I promised I wouldn't. But,' she added hopefully, 'it would be all right if you came with me.'

He looked out across the dark sea. 'Well, not right now, I think. Another time perhaps. What brought you out, Pen? The heat?'

'The heat?' She sounded astonished. 'Heavens, no. The noise—the sound of a motor boat.' She looked up at him and in the moonlight he could see that her face was serious, even a little worried.

She turned away from him. 'Well, it's silly but you

73

see, I thought it was Stu's boat. He often went there at night recently.'

'What for?'

He saw the flash of her wide grin as she said, *'Cherchez la femme.'*

'Good heavens. Moonlight assignations? Are you sure?'

'No. Well yes, pretty sure.'

'Did they meet there or go together?'

'They met there. I used to hear two boats.'

He was astounded. 'Penny, why on earth didn't you say so before?'

'I keep telling you,' she said impatiently, 'to find out who it was.'

'You can't be sure it was a woman in the other boat.'

'No, I can't. But I have my reasons.'

He jammed his hands into his pockets and walked on. 'Penny, you asked me to help in this case, but you are holding back. What do you know that you haven't told?'

*'Nothing.* But you know Stu has had a sun room made in the ruins of the old house. There's no running water or electricity but there are Lilos and cushions and a paraffin stove. And it's *very* romantic.'

'And very inconvenient I'd have thought.'

'Then you haven't thought very far,' she retorted. 'Or you've never had an affair with a married woman.'

He shot her a look. 'Not everybody does.'

'No. But can't you see how difficult it must be if you live alone with a manservant? You've either got to let him know everything like he's a sort of Figaro or you have to creep about in your own house, pretending you're alone when you're not. On King's Rock they were safe.'

'Away from prying eyes,' he mocked.

She grimaced wryly. 'I didn't pry, I notice things, I never pried. I just knew it was happening. And Stu didn't stop me going to King's Rock whenever I liked, so perhaps he didn't mind if I did know. Because he'd know I wouldn't talk and I wouldn't have —ever. Only now it's different.'

'Yes, it is,' he said sombrely. 'I don't suppose Stu was murdered by his girl friend, but he could have been blackmailed about her.'

They walked on in silence for a moment.

'But why,' she said suddenly, 'did *Stu* get killed? You don't kill the goose that lays the golden eggs.'

'Of course not.' They reached to top of the zig-zag where they could look down on Port King and its tiny harbour, and by tacit consent they stopped and Susie, silent as a mole, stopped too.

Down in the cove all was quiet. A small dim light shone in the house, the moon lit up the inlet and glimmered on the launch anchored in its usual place.

Clive spoke softly. 'Stu's boat is there.'

'Yes.' Penny stared down into the quiet cove. 'It must have been the other boat.'

'If there was one.'

She looked at him seriously. 'You don't believe me.'

'I think you were dreaming,' he said gently. 'You've heard it before, you thought you heard it again. I was awake and I didn't hear it. Neither, apparently, did the policeman on duty at Port King.'

'No, that's true.' She shrugged and turning

75

abruptly, began to walk back towards King's View. 'All right, if you won't come swimming, let's not waste any more time.'

In silence they walked back over the gentle springy turf, enveloped in a night so beautiful that it was almost unbelievable to him. That violence had ever touched this quiet place.

He opened the front door for Penny and Susie with a nod of appreciation walked in ahead of them.

'Good night, Pen.' Clive felt she was disappointed but could offer her little comfort. 'You may be right about the girl friend. I'll try to find out.'

She turned back to look at him. 'Aren't you coming in?'

'I think I'll have a cigarette first. I'll let you know if I hear any motor boats.'

It struck him then that Stuart—or his girl friend if she existed—might have made good use of a silent motor boat.

.   .   .   .   .

Despite attempts to keep the funeral quiet, a lot of people attended it. Stuart had been well-known in the district, had employed a number of people in his boatyards, had been a small-time squire in his own locality. Not everyone who came could be accused of curiosity.

Clive devoted most of his time to Stuart's cousin and heir who had arrived just in time and was planning to leave again almost immediately. He was only vaguely aware of Maria giving both moral and physical support to Rowena; of Clare pale and beautiful standing near to an equally pale and drawn-looking Michael; of Superintendent Marshall fading into the background and of Penny, her hair flaming in the sun and accompanying, of all people, Blanes.

There is, he discovered, little comfort to be gained from the words of the funeral service when they are said over the body of a man relentlessly murdered by a fellow human being.

And by now Stuart's death was not only being treated as murder, it was *known* to be so. Superintendent Marshall was no longer pretending to be keeping an eye on the case only because the dead man was rich and influential. He was firmly in charge now, reporting back to his superiors without diffidence and ready to acknowledge that it might soon be necessary to ask for help from Scotland Yard.

He told Clive some of this as, after the funeral, they went back to Port King together. The Superintendent wanted to be present when Clive opened a small safe, the code of which he had only just obtained.

The contents of the safe got them no further however. There were a few pieces of jewellery, a number of old deeds, a small sheaf of elderly looking papers.

Clive flipped through them. 'They all appear to be at least twenty years old—probably from Stuart's mother's time. Stu mostly used the big more modern safe in his study. But John Tredger, his solicitor, is going up to King's View for tea. I'll take them up and we'll study them and let you know what they are.'

The Superintendent nodded. 'Twenty years ago lets Highstone out. He'd have been a nine-year-old child.'

'By the way'—against his will Clive found himself asking the question—'do you know where he was last night. In one of your—er—guest rooms?'

'He's been promoted,' said the Superintendent. 'Got a room over the café on the quay. The café's kept by Constable Miller's sister.'

'Could he have been out last night?'

The Superintendent looked startled. 'I'd doubt it. Why?'

'Miss Keats thought she heard a motor boat out near King's Rock. *I* didn't hear it and neither, apparently, did your man on duty at the entrance of Port King. I just wondered . . .'

'I don't think it could have been Highstone. But I'll check. And, of course, we haven't put King's Rock out of bounds—any boat owner can take a trip round the bay if he feels like it.'

'Yes, I know.' Clive shrugged his shoulders. 'I think she imagined it anyway—she used to hear King's boat at night and she probably heard it again in a dream.'

The Superintendent nodded.

'And talking of angels or speaking of the devil Miss Keats now appears to be about to commandeer King's boat.'

'She's probably inspecting it for fingerprints,' said Clive watching Penny's lordly assumption of authority with some amusement. He glanced at the Superintendent who smiled and nodded.

'Yes, we've been over it thoroughly.'

'By the way,' said Clive abruptly, 'may I go to King's Rock?'

Superintendent Marshall's eyebrows shot up. 'Is that what you think Miss Keats has in mind?'

78

'I've no idea,' said Clive resignedly, 'what Miss Keats has in mind. I'll go and ask her.'

'Well, you can go to the Rock,' said the Superintendent, 'and you can use the boat. We've got a mass of fingerprints from King's Rock, but I'm sure they'll all prove to belong to Mr. King's friends. He was killed out doors, not in the sun room.'

Clive went to join Penny on the jetty where she was sitting, looking despondently down at the boat. He sat down beside her.

'The Superintendent wants to know what's in your mind.'

She smiled but it was not her usual uninhibited grin. 'He needn't worry.'

'Then I,' he said more seriously, 'would like to know what's *on* your mind.'

'Rowena,' she said without looking at him.

'Rowena!'

'I think it was Rowena.'

After a moment he said gently, 'You've found out something?'

'No, not really.' She lifted a handful of dusty sand that she had been piling up with her fingers and shook it back on to the jetty. 'But she's behaving very oddly.'

Instinctively he glanced up at the cliff above them, to where Rowena was probably still taking tea and making small talk with Maria.

'I don't think so. She's an emotional sort of woman. On the whole she was calmer than I expected her to be.'

Penny shook her head. 'She is making the most tremendous effort to *appear* calm. And that's worrying. For one thing why should she be so much more

79

upset than we are? And if she is upset because she's the easily upset type, why should she try to hide it? She looks dreadful, she's having a very bad time. But *we* are the ones who Stu was friendly with. So far as we know Rowena was only an acquaintance.'

'What else?' he asked as she lapsed again into an unusual silence, her brown fingers still busy with the silvery sand.

'Rowena would—does—wear tights on the beach. Rowena could—probably does—use loose powder. She's rich, she's about Stu's age, she's married, she would hate a scandal. She's left alone a great deal —George is rarely home and most of the time she's alone in that big soulless house just her and her car and her motor boat that's the same model as Stuart's. And she took it very badly when you told us Stu was dead. I'd forgotten that but I remembered today when I saw her at the funeral. And she knew he couldn't swim, which only his close friends did.'

Having blurted this out as if she were unloading a great burden, she was silent again, waiting for him to speak. When he did it was with some reluctance.

'You're very convincing.'

She turned and looked at him quickly, her expression serious.

'In fact,' he went on, 'I think you may be right. Even so, if we knew she was the *femme* for whom you've been so assiduously searching, it doesn't mean she hit Stu over the head and pushed him in the sea.'

'No,' she agreed. 'But it leads to unpleasant deductions.'

'Penny,' he said seriously, 'I warned you about this. If you try to prove someone is innocent, you may only succeed in proving him guilty. But if you

80

prove him innocent you prove someone else is guilty. You can't have your criminal and eat your cake. You've insisted on uncovering things and now you've got to accept what you've uncovered.'

'All *I've* done,' said Penny despondently, 'is throw doubts on the morals of a woman I wish no harm to. I haven't uncovered a thing.'

He got to his feet. 'Oh yes you have,' he said. 'And I'm off to London first thing in the morning to make an enquiry or two.'

.　　.　　.　　.　　.

Henry Longmore, the managing director of Michael's firm, was surprised but co-operative.

Yes, he valued Michael highly as a draughtsman; not a man of great initiative but hard-working, keen and a splendid technician. Yes, they'd be delighted if he was back in the job in a day or two.

'And if he's charged?'

Mr. Longmore folded his large hands on the desk and looked at Clive over his glasses. 'Do you think there's any danger?'

'It's possible,' said Clive.

An old-fashioned ship's clock ticked noisily on the wall.

'Then we shall help him,' said Mr. Longmore at length.

Clive let out a small sigh of relief.

'Good. Now, do you mind if I ask a few questions? This silent engine of yours—'

Mr. Longmore winced and Clive hesitated.

'It's not secret?' he asked anxiously.

'No it's not, though we prefer that it shouldn't be publicly discussed.'

'Could anyone buy the idea from Michael?'

Mr. Longmore looked astonished. 'Of course not. It's ours—it's his special project but he's carried it out on our behalf.'

'Could Stuart King have bought it?'

'He wouldn't want it. He bought our engines and one day I suppose he might have bought a Longmore-Silent for his own use. But he wasn't in that sort of trade.'

'Would you sell the idea?'

'To someone bigger than ourselves perhaps.'

'For a lot of money?'

'Yes.'

'What would £2,000 buy?'

Mr. Longmore laughed. 'Nothing. Except perhaps Michael's spare time.'

'But he—Highstone *could* have sold the idea.'

'He is much too sensible,' said Mr. Longmore with a small smile, 'to sell an idea so cheaply.'

As he spoke, his eyes darkened and his voice dropped away.

Clive waited.

'What makes you think Michael was selling anything?' Mr. Longmore's tone had changed again. Once more he was brisk.

'I don't think, I just wonder. King was quite a rich man.'

The other man shook his head. 'Not as rich as that.'

'Rich as what?'

'To buy the idea—either from us openly or from Michael under the counter.'

'*Is* it such a good idea? Is it really a marketable product?'

'In a small way.'

'Who wants a silent motor boat? Why does it matter?'

Mr. Longmore's long fingers clasped themselves again, and he sat back. This was the kind of talk he enjoyed and the moment of doubt had passed.

'Well, of course, it's a limited market but there are always people who will buy the best and this will be in a class of its own. There are the genuine noise-haters. Michael is one of them which is why he likes the project. Then, of course, these days there are a lot of people living on the quays of tiny crowded harbours, or even on launches near a lot of other launches. Motor boats bringing people home from parties in the middle of the night can be disturbing. We'll have a reasonable sale on the big sailing estuaries. If we can make a bigger engine do the same job, some of the more luxurious pleasure-boat firms will like it. Easier for the guides to give their running commentaries. And, I'm afraid, there will always be the smugglers.'

'Smugglers!'

Even as he repeated the old romanticized word Clive was reminded of Penny. 'Smugglers,' she had said. 'They were shot and wounded and died in the coves.' And now in this civilized place talking to a highly civilized man the word, ancient and un-civilized, had come up again. What had the civilized, thoughtful, law-abiding Stuart had to do with that nefarious trade?

Feeling the need to go away and think he began

83

to make his farewells. But Mr. Longmore seemed disinclined to let him go.

'Can you not stay to lunch? We have an excellent canteen.'

Clive shook his head. 'Thank you but I must get on to London.'

'A drink then?' Without waiting for an answer he rose and went over to a cabinet by the window. 'What will it be?'

'Whiskey, please.' Clive rose too and followed him across the room, attracted by the enormous plate glass window that almost constituted a fourth wall. 'My God, you've got a view here.'

Below them was the river, spreading out into the estuary, wide and open and dappled with sunshine. It was as different as possible from the trees and coves of Merrynmouth, and yet it was, in its solid commercial way, almost as beautiful.

*Clare will love it.* The thought popped unbidden into his mind and he stood still for a moment while pangs of misery assailed him. Without a struggle, without so much as a word of argument, in his mind he had lost her. He stared out across the grey and silver estuary, busy about its own strange rituals, and he knew the depths of despair.

'May I ask,' said the cool precise tones of Mr. Longmore, consumed with curiosity yet determined not to appear curious, 'just what is your role in this affair?'

'Friend of the suspect, I suppose you might say,' Clive answered at random with a kind of bitterness.

'But you hardly know him.' Mr. Longmore put a drink in his hand and pulled two chairs up to the window.

'I believe he is innocent,' said Clive.

'And the police do not?'

'As a matter of fact I believe they do. And I suspect that they will very shortly prove it to themselves. In which case I shall have wasted my time and yours.'

'I think not,' said Mr. Longmore in his quiet even voice. 'I think you are trying to prove Michael is not only innocent of murder but innocent of anything else. You are trying to prove him—what's the expression—clean?'

*More fool me* ran through Clive's mind as he lifted his glass. It was hardly the answer he could give this courteous man. 'Perhaps,' he allowed.

'Well, we—my partners and I—appreciate that. Michael is a valued employee. Whatever the outcome we shall try to help him. But the more positively he is cleared, naturally the happier we shall be. I hope that one day he will come on the board as technical director,' went on Mr. Longmore.

*That will make him an even more suitable husband for Clare.* Clive took another sip of his drink and felt the whiskey flare through him. He was tired, hungry and depressed and the drink was acting on every nerve in his body. I'm going mad, he thought. I must stop this nonsense.

'Superintendent Marshall telephoned me,' said Mr. Longmore unexpectedly.

'To tell you I had his permission to come?' Clive smiled.

'Yes.' He paused. 'I didn't know the police used outside help.'

'Have you never heard of Sherlock Holmes?' Clive asked mockingly and then was ashamed of him-

85

self. 'Sometimes they do. Obviously they have to use experts in certain specialized fields. My field is security. I've worked with the police here and with Interpol. Never a civil case before though. They're —indulging me.'

'You do not appear to be enjoying it much, if you'll forgive my saying so. And the Superintendent gave me a different impression. He implied that your methods are more subtle than his men's might be.'

'Not always,' Clive put down his glass and stood up. 'What is on your mind?'

For a long moment the other man stared out at the vastness outside, twirling the glass in his hand. Clive waited.

'That £2,000,' Mr. Longmore said at last. 'It could have been a loan?'

'It could. Only Michael claims he knew nothing about it, but it could have been payment *for* a loan couldn't it? Isn't that what's in your mind?'

'Yes,' Mr. Longmore turned to him with obvious relief and took a long gulp of his drink.

'Payment for lending the prototype.'

'*One* of the prototypes. There are two models in existence. One is Michael's own; kept in his own boathouse. The other is ours. We agreed to this because we believe there should always be a substitute model in case of accidents and because it gives a designer a chance to make changes to one while leaving the other as a control.'

'£2,000,' said Clive carefully, 'is a lot of money to pay for the hire of a motor boat.'

'Yes,' agreed Mr. Longmore. 'You would have to want it very badly indeed.'

.　　.　　.　　.　　.

London was hot and sticky and exhausting. Clive, making his way through the sizzling streets, felt that it was an entirely different place from the one he had left only a few days earlier. He was a stranger, a man with a load of mischief.

He had telephoned for an appointment before leaving the Estuary so no barriers were put between him and the man he wanted to see.

'I'm sorry,' he said coming straight to the point, 'to be breaking in on your working day like this but I need some information about possible smuggling activities.'

'Where?' The other man was no waster of words. He turned to a wall-sized map of the country and handed Clive a long pointed stick.

Merrynmouth looked not only small and insignificant, it looked a most unlikely place for the big deals of present-day smugglers. Clive pointed to it and waited for his companion's comment.

'Hm. Traditional. Brandy for the parson, but not the modern stuff. Hasn't been a bad report for years.'

He picked up another long stick and pointed. 'Drugs here sometimes. And the odd case of brandy here—and there. Illegal immigrants all down this coast here. Watches and cameras there. But your place is too tricky for landing and it's difficult to get anything bulky out of the coves. Still you never know, we'll look into it.'

.    .    .    .    .

Despite the lateness of the hour and the long journey, Clive decided to go back to King's View that night. He phoned Superintendent Marshall who asked him to call in, whatever time he arrived. He had something important to say, something he obviously considered more important than anything Clive could tell him, and when Clive arrived he came straight to the point.

'Highstone isn't with us any longer. He's still staying, on his own decision at the café, but not as our guest.'

'He's clear?'

The Superintendent raised his eyebrows. 'I didn't say that. But we've found a couple of people who remember seeing him on the way down so I don't reckon he *could* have been here at the time of the murder. We can pick him up again if we need to.'

Clive nodded. 'I'm sure you're right. I'll go and see him.'

'I think,' said the Superintendent suddenly diffident, 'that you'll find him up at King's View.'

Clive nodded again. 'Do you want me to tell you what *I* found out?'

Marshall grinned. 'What do you think?'

.　　.　　.　　.　　.

'Hello,' said Penny. 'How did you get on?'

'I'm not sure. Get me a drink and I'll tell you.'

'The whiskey,' said her cool young voice out of the shadow, 'is on the table. And there are sandwiches. I'm glad you've come. I was beginning to eat them myself.'

She was sitting on the terrace, Susie at her feet. There was no sign of Clare and Michael, or even of Maria.

Clive poured himself a drink.

88

'Cheers. Where are the others?'

'Maria went to dinner with Rowena. She's very late; I expect she'll be home soon. There's been a bit of action here: Michael has left the police station.'

'Yes, I know. I saw Superintendent Marshall. But I understand he's still staying in the village.'

'Yes. But right now he's out with Clare.'

'I see. Well you know I'm not especially surprised.'

'What did you find out?' she asked, deliberately stiff.

He hesitated, then said, 'You won't like it.'

She sighed. 'I'm getting used to situations I don't like.'

'I rather think Stuart may have been smuggling.'

'*Smuggling!* Stu?'

'It looks like it.'

She struggled with the idea for several seconds before she said reluctantly, 'Well I see why you might think it. King's Rock is a perfect landing place, and he has been going there at night. But what would he smuggle and why? And what does Michael have to do with it?'

'I don't know what he smuggled. I don't *know* that he did it at all. But it would explain a lot that we haven't been able to understand. As for Michael, well I'm going to see him tomorrow.'

There was a long silence. The night was very still and the moon was not yet up. He could not see her clearly but he knew that she was trying, as she always did, to assimilate his new and unwelcome idea, to rationalize, it and equate it with all she already knew. He felt a sudden wave of admiration for someone so young who was so determinedly reasonable. No excess of emotion for her, he thought with something like envy. Test everything with your brain, your quite considerable brain.

'Well,' she said at length, 'you warned me I might not like what you turned up. I don't.'

'No, neither do I.'

'What is more,' she said firmly, 'I don't believe it. So now, Clive dear, you not only have to prove Michael isn't a murderer, you also have to prove Stuart was not a smuggler.'

For a moment he could not believe his ears. Then he smiled. 'And I was just thinking what a sane, logical creature you are.'

'There is nothing insane or illogical about that. Have you told Superintendent Marshall what you think?'

'No. It *is* only a suspicion at the moment. But if my pal at the Customs and Excise comes up with anything definite I shall have to tell him. I only told you because you seem to know a good deal about Stu's activities and I thought you might react.'

'Well, I've reacted.' She leant forward to pick up a sandwich and he saw her face in the pool of light from the house. 'I don't like it.' She looked up and caught his glance. 'I'm a dissatisfied sort of customer, aren't I, not liking anything you serve up. I don't like the idea of Stuart and Rowena, and I like this even less. But you can't stop now.'

'No. Let's have the truth.'

He got suddenly to his feet as a car came up the drive and stopped outside the stables.

'It's Maria,' said Penny.

He shot her a look which she did not see and walked to the end of the terrace to meet Maria.

'Oh you're back.' She did not sound pleased. 'I wondered if you'd stay the night.'

'I don't like London in a heatwave. Did you have a good evening?'

'Well,' Maria sat down and accepted a cigarette. 'Hello, Pen—it was delicious food and George's best Hock but I think Rowena's been terribly frightened by poor Stuart's death. She didn't seem to want me to leave, which is why I'm so late. And she's talking of leaving Merrynmouth and going to live nearer London.'

There was an uneasy silence while both her listeners digested and analysed these random remarks.

Maria herself became uneasy. 'Is Clare in bed? Or is she still out.'

'Still out,' Penny answered quickly. 'I don't suppose she'll be long now.'

Clive said nothing. Watching the glow of his cigarette Maria suddenly recalled the moment when she had first seen Michael walking across the grass with Clare and had unaccountably feared for the future. And now she was even more afraid—afraid for her daughter, afraid for the man who sat so silently beside her.

Penny said her good nights, whistled up Susie and went to her room. Maria felt she must either go too or she must talk, putting into words all that she was thinking and feeling about Clare, about Michael, about Clive. But instinct told her such words would not be welcome, that the time had not come either for motherly chats or for condemnation. Rather than say the wrong thing, she went to bed too.

The night was still warm, there was still some

91

whiskey in the decanter and cigarettes in the silver box that Penny, a militant non-smoker, had put out for him. Clive waited.

At five o'clock with a brilliant sun coming up behind the house and a sky washed clear of cloud he went to bed. Clare had not come home.

.    .    .    .    .

Clive was out of the house before eight o'clock that morning and by the time he returned from Merrynmouth Clare was eating breakfast on the lawn. She looked up from her newspaper and smiled at him.

With wonder he realized that her face was composed as ever. There was no sign of strain or anxiety; she was serene and happy. Only when she studied his face did a tiny flicker of apprehension cross her own.

His heart thumping, he thought wryly, it would serve you right, my girl, if I fell to the ground in a spasm.

'Where have you come from?' she asked.

'The sea,' he said.

'Did you come home last night?'

'Yes.' But *you* did not, *you* did not, *you* did not.

'How did you get on?'

He had expected almost anything but that. 'I don't know yet,' he replied evenly. 'I need to see Michael.'

'He's staying with Constable Miller's sister, in a room over her teashop.'

'Is it comfortable?'

'Yes, very.'

*More comfortable than the sand below the cliff?* Stop it, Clive, stop it.

He said, 'I'll go down to see him as soon as I've had some of that coffee.'

'Sorry.' She passed him a cup. 'I'll get you some breakfast. What would you like?'

'That toast will do.'

She felt it. 'It's hard.'

'Never mind.' He took it. 'So is life.'

'Yes,' she said seriously, 'it is.'

She raised her eyes to his. 'I'm sorry, Clive. I'm terribly, terribly sorry if it hurts you but this is *it*. This is what I've been waiting for for twenty-six years.'

He spread the toast thickly with butter.

'We'll see,' he said. 'Give it a little time.'

She shook her head. 'I *know*.'

'Well, wait a few days. Let's get this business cleared up before you really decide. See what happens.'

Her eyes filled with tears. 'But don't you see, I don't *care* what happens. Whatever you find out, I'm committed.'

'Not publicly. Please, Clare,' he put out his hand and covered her own, 'don't take any irrevocable steps for just a few more days. Then we'll discuss it.'

'There's really nothing to discuss.' She took her hand away and though she did it gently, it was as if she had hit him. 'But all right, a few days. And then we must tell people.'

He covered the thickly buttered toast with marmalade and threw it carefully to the gulls which swooped and fluttered a few yards from the table.

'Thank you.' He got to his feet. 'I'm going to see Michael now. And then probably the Superintendent. Do you happen to know where Penny is?'

She shook her head. 'Probably swimming. You didn't see her in the cove?'

'I swam from the village,' he said, and smiled, 'I'm still not as tough as Penny.'

.        .        .        .        .

Penny had wakened early that morning to an unaccountable feeling of gloom. It was a blackness so unlike the cheerful anticipation with which she normally greeted a new day that instead of getting up immediately as she usually did, she lay in bed trying to fathom the reason for it.

It was something that had happened yesterday making her feel like this. No—something Clive had said last night! His only half-serious suggestion that Stuart might have been smuggling.

It had come as a complete surprise to her but now she knew that even as she slept a bell had been ringing in her mind. Tucked away in her memory was a fragment of knowledge that made Clive's supposition just a little more likely.

She got out of bed and went to the window. The sea danced and glittered in the morning sun. There was no hint of the sinister, the shady, the suspicious to be seen; the day, the place, were blandly smiling. But out of sight was the zig-zag path that the old smugglers had used; and the dark trees growing down the cove almost to the edge of the shore where the vast rocks took over the job of providing cover. And on the black rock island, less than half a mile away, hidden from sight and known to only a few people was Penny's little bit of secret information. Was it still there, that secret Stuart had shared

94

with her? Or was it gone, as he had told her all those years ago, it soon would be?

She splashed herself violently with cold water by way of a wash, pulled on her swimsuit and shorts, slid her arms into a thin shirt and her feet into espadrilles, and crept along the passage to Clive's room.

When he did not reply to her discreet knock, she gently opened the door and was confronted by an empty room.

Downstairs she silenced an ecstatic Susie who considered the household always slept too late and they made their way together down the zig-zag.

She had been confident that she would find Clive there but the little beach was empty and there was no sign of a swimmer. She turned to glance back at Port King but the house had a shuttered and silent look.

Blanes' boat was moored in the inlet and for a moment she was tempted to take it and go over to King's Rock at once. But resisting that temptation she fell for the blandishments of the cool silver sea and went swimming instead.

She could quite easily have swum to the rock this morning. The water was calm, the tide low. But something held her back; it would be better if she could first tell Clive what was on her mind.

A little reluctantly she turned her back on the island and swam slowly into shore. Susie, a furiously enthusiastic swimmer, wallowed beside her. In the cove one of the tall rocks threw a shadow on to the smooth tide-washed sand and in the shadow stood a man.

For a moment a little spark of fear shot through

her and she turned her head to see where Susie was. The little dog, showing no signs of dismay, was ploughing on towards the sand. Penny telling herself not to be a fool, did the same.

It was only when she reached the shallows and could stand up that she was able to shade her eyes from the dazzle of sun and sea and sky and recognize the figure waiting so quietly in the shadow. He was sitting now on a flat rock, and was clearly waiting for her.

'Blanes!' She ran through the tiny waves, pushing her wet hair back. 'What are you doing here, you scared me.'

'You scared *me*,' he grumbled, handing her a towel he had brought from the house. 'You shouldn't do it, you really shouldn't, not till they know what happened to poor Mr. Stuart.'

'Oh nonsense!' She rubbed her face and head violently. 'Anyway I'm rather glad to see you. I want to borrow your boat.'

'We'll talk about that over breakfast,' he said. 'There's enough for two spoiling in the oven.'

'Oh!' she put out a hand and pulled the old man to his feet. 'You're a lovely man, and I'm very hungry.'

The look of pleasure on his face cut her to the quick. The poor old thing, the poor lonely frightened old thing.

But being Penny she was brisk with him. The first pangs of hunger staved off, she extracted from him what she wanted.

'It's not mine to lend,' he grumbled, when she asked for his boat. ' 'Tis Mr. Stuart's.'

'Yours to use till the heir demands it,' she said crisply.

'And how would you know that?'

'I'm friends with the executor.'

He contemplated this for a moment, drinking his tea in a gentleman's gentlemanly way. 'Well all right, if you'll promise to do nothing reckless.'

'You can trust me.'

'Can I?' he said darkly.

'And the inside keys to King's Rock.'

'You'll not be going there on your own now.'

'Not if I can get Clive to go with me.'

'Well, he's the boss now till the new one takes over. You can have them for him.'

She looked at him across the little kitchen table and said gently: 'What are your plans, Blanes? A life of luxury on what Stu left you?'

'He's been generous,' he answered, 'but what would I be doing with a life of leisure? I'll be looking for work, my dear!'

He looked old and unhappy and the day dulled before her eyes.

'Where?'

'I was wondering,' he said, his eyes on hers, 'if Mr. Richards and Miss Greatly could be doing with me.'

She picked up her cup to hide her face. She could not bring herself to tell him of her own doubts about Clive and Clare.

'They may not take a place here,' she said at length. 'Mr. Richards has to be in London such a lot.'

'I thought I might try it.'

'London! Oh, Blanes, you'd hate it.'

'I like him,' he said, getting up to fetch the teapot from the stove.

She was silent. She was desperately sorry for him

and it was quite impossible to explain that young married couples—even supposing this particular young couple ever got married—no longer included elderly menservants as part of their households. It was hard to see Clive needing a Jeeves.

'Perhaps my aunt,' she said at last with a small sigh, 'could afford you.'

'I'd need only my board and keep,' he said. 'Have you had enough to eat?'

By the time she had eaten another round of toast, drunk another cup of tea and returned to King's View, Clive had been back and had left again.

.    .    .    .    .

On his way to find Michael, Clive was careful to keep his mind on the main problem and not to think about the forthcoming interview. He had been trained to converse socially with men he was about to trap; to carry on an equable relationship with men he knew to be trying to trap him; to entrusting worthless secrets to men he suspected of being untrustworthy; and to maintaining friendly relations with men he knew to be enemies. But never before had he gone to so much trouble for a man who had caused him so much anguish.

He was confident of his own ability to handle the situation. He was not at all sure how Michael would manage it.

The café over which Superintendent Marshall had so cleverly manipulated Michael was on the old fishing quay. This morning in the continuing bright sunshine the whole area was busy with boating holidaymakers, boat-owners, and fishermen. Only Michael seemed still—a solitary figure on one of the old wooden seats dotted along the quayside. He caught sight of Clive as he approached and his expression was one of pleased surprise. He rose gracefully to his feet and spoke first.

'So you're back. We didn't expect you till later today.'

'I came back last night.' Clive dropped the words casually and waited.

'You're not having much of a holiday, are you?' said Michael.

He appeared to speak with genuine concern. It was a bit breathtaking really, Clive thought, and he sat down abruptly on the seat and said, 'We may as well talk here if it suits you.'

'What sort of day did you have? Did you get anywhere?' Michael sat down and he was clearly trying to appear rather more casual than he felt. Clive was surprised to find himself wishing he had something positive, something encouraging to say. He was not the detective in this case; he was the advocate. He had set out to try and prove this young man's innocence, and while all his instincts and training had taught him to keep an open mind, to secrete his information away, to keep his thoughts to himself, he was aware that he could be of no help to Michael if he did not put at least some of his cards on the table. It was no use being half-hearted about a mission, however reluctant one had been to undertake it.

'Just once more,' he said carefully, 'are you quite sure you can think of no reason why Stuart should have been going to offer you money?'

'No.'

'Have you *tried* to think or have you closed your mind to it?'

'Of course I've tried to think,' Michael said with a sudden show of irritation. 'I've thought and thought but for God's sake, Clive, I barely knew the man, how can I tell what was in his possibly devious mind? Ever since you came up from that bloody beach that day—when was it—last week, a lifetime ago?—I've been number one suspect in a crime I know nothing about. Maybe I'm not thinking as clearly as I should, maybe I'm not really thinking at all, only worrying. But by God I *am* worried and so would you be in my shoes.'

He stopped, waiting for an answer.

Clive said nothing. The sun sent off splashes of light on the faintly rippling water. The friendly sounds of boats, arriving, pushing off, bumping gently together, mingled with contented summer voices made a background to the strained silence between them. In the end it was Michael who broke it.

'Sorry,' he said briefly.

Clive nodded. 'That's all right. Now answer a more difficult one. Would you—*could* you have *lent* Stuart your silent prototype? The one in your own boathouse, not the factory one?'

For a moment he thought there was to be another outburst and a more violent one. But after the first swift gesture of denial Michael leant back against the seat, only his expression indicating the struggle within him.

'I wouldn't,' he said eventually. 'But I suppose I *could* have. Do you think . . . ?'

'I don't know what to think,' said Clive.

He knew he sounded weary and wished that he didn't. But Michael's face suddenly lost its look of self-abstraction and he looked at Clive penetratingly.

'I think you've thought a good bit further than *I* have,' he said. 'I think you've got something.' He suddenly swept a brown hand over his sunburnt face and for a moment the dark eyes were closed. 'I've been such a fool,' he said quietly, 'such a fool. Of course that's what he wanted.'

A small shiver ran through Clive. He'd experienced this before, this tiny change in the course of events, the first small breakthrough before the showdown.

'You've remembered something?'

'Yes, yes, he asked how far the tests had gone and whether it was in a shape for passengers and if she was seaworthy. He even asked if I'd ever tried it in waters like these—you know, coves and bays and rock hazards, where you're twisting and turning. I got the impression that one day he'd invite me to bring her round the coast and give her a few trials from his boatyards. But I didn't take it seriously and anyway at the time we were talking she wasn't ready for a long trip.'

'Is she now?'

'Yes.'

'So you might have been persuaded?'

'I might. But what has two thousand pounds to do with persuasion?'

Clive smiled. 'He didn't know what kind of man you were any more than you knew what kind of man he was. He wanted that boat.'

'But what *for*?'

Clive got to his feet. 'That's what I've got to find

out. It helps to know he wanted it. I'll see you later.'

'Where are you off to?'

'To visit his boatyards along the coast, find out what his managers know.'

'Can I come?'

'Better not,' said Clive. His tone was impersonal but Michael flushed.

'No of course not. You know, I keep forgetting who I am.' He stood up and for a moment Clive glimpsed what Penny had recognised—the diffident man behind the handsome, confident front.

'I do realize, you know, what you're doing for me. And I'll never be able to repay you—or thank you enough.'

The enormity of this caused Clive to stop in his tracks and turn back. For once he felt inclined to speak what was in his mind or fling this incredible young man into the sparkling water behind him. But he did neither. He only smiled slightly and said, 'Don't speak too soon,' and was gone.

Michael went back to the seat and watched the gradual speeding up of the quayside life. There was really nothing else for him to do until Clare joined him, which he was sure she would.

A small motor boat came expertly up to the quayside and a voice called, 'Catch.' He caught the mooring rope, tied up the boat and watched as Penny, followed inevitably by Susie, climbed up the steps to the quay.

'Good morning. Have you seen Clive?'

'He left me a few minutes ago in that classy monster of his.'

'Where was he going?'

'Along the coast to visit the King boatyards.'

102

'Damn.' Penny looked at her watch. 'And the tide's against me, I'd never catch him up by sea.'

'Is it important?' Michael grinned slightly at her furious concern. He felt a little shy with this young woman, and not at all as if he knew her, despite the hours that he had spent at King's View.

'It could be. Well, it will have to wait.' Penny was not one to waste time worrying over what could not be helped, and her face resumed its normal expression of enjoyable expectancy.

She looked across at where the little café was beginning to come to life and said: 'I'll buy you a coffee, we can drink it out here.' Marching purposefully over to the door, she called out: 'Hilda, two coffees, please, for me and your lodger. And we'll have it on the *Rue de la Paix*,' and picking up a small table carried it to the quayside, anchored a dark cloth with two sugar basins and despatched Michael for chairs. Hilda who, far from resenting this take-over seemed to be enjoying it, promptly produced two cups of coffee and the bill which she thrust into Penny's hand. 'There you are, otherwise Mr. Highstone might take it.'

'This is very gentlemanly of you, Penny.' Michael sat down at the table with a sudden feeling of relaxation. Perhaps this girl wasn't as formidable as she seemed. But after her burst of activity, she was suddenly quiet, sitting with her elbows on the table, both hands round her cup, her face thoughtful. He sat back and watched her, conscious that though no one in their senses could compare her to Clare, she had her own brand of distinction that made passersby glance at her with interest. This would not, in other circumstances, he thought grimly, be an un-

103

pleasant way of passing a beautiful summer morning.

She echoed his thoughts with uncanny accuracy. 'Isn't it sickening,' she said suddenly, 'that after all that cold and rain we're getting weather like this and none of us can enjoy it. I'll bet you anything the day it's all cleared up, the weather will change.'

'You do think it's going to be cleared up then?'

She put down her cup and tilted her face to the cloudless sky. 'Yes, I do. But the waiting and the flogging it out is ghastly. And instead of being able to enjoy all this you must be wishing you'd never heard of Merrynmouth.'

'No,' he said thoughtfully. 'Always provided I get out of the mess I'm in I'll always be glad I came. If I hadn't I wouldn't have met Clare.'

Michael was not an over-sensitive man but he knew at once that the atmosphere had changed. He had been basking in the unexpected warmth of Penny's friendship. Now she was looking at him from a great distance and he was amazed again at how remarkably formidable she could be. But it did not last. It was Penny herself who broke the ice and her tone was more inquiring than aggressive.

'Do you honestly not know that Clare is engaged to Clive?'

She knew at once that he had not. He looked as if she had struck him which indeed for a moment she could have done. And she saw, too, that she had put him in an intolerably difficult position from which it was only fair to rescue him. But first she must know what he had to say.

When he spoke he chose his words carefully.

'I know, of course, that they have been—very

104

close. I didn't know they were ever engaged. Are you sure?'

It was at that moment that Penny gave up the struggle to bring Clive and Clare together again. If Clive could get her back, well and good. If he couldn't, this man would do. She felt she had set him the key question in a fatal examination and he had answered it and should be allowed to live. He had thrown doubts on Penny's information: he had avoided casting any aspersion on Clare.

So she forebore to say that the engagement was of six months' duration and that the marriage was planned for later in the year. She did not tell him that one of the purposes of this holiday at King's View was to discuss such undoubted facts as where to go on the honeymoon, whether to keep on Clive's flat or try to find a house, whether they should be married in London or Merrynmouth. Instead she said simply, 'I'm sorry, it's none of my business. I shouldn't have spoken.'

He stared down into his coffee cup. 'I've been a bloody fool, Penny. I should have known. And Clive . . . is flogging round the country on my business . . .'

'He knows,' she said quietly. 'He knows you've fallen for Clare. He's doing it regardless.'

'But *I* didn't know, that's what's so awful.' He got up impatiently, almost violently. 'Another coffee . . .'

And while he was gone Penny did a little more fast growing up. What Clare had done was unforgivable—and had to be forgiven. Directness and honesty which seemed so desirable could be hurtful and offensive. The people one loved were not always per-

105

fect; Clare had faults, even Clive had faults, even Clive, even Clive, even Clive . . .

In her mind's eye she could see him now behind the wheel of his classy monster; taut, unhappy, determined. He must have faults because he was a human being but *she* could not see them.

'Oh Lor!' said Penny to herself and sat quietly in the warmth of the sun facing a new, surprising and unpalatable fact of life.

By the time Michael returned to the table she had assimilated that fact and was prepared to live with it. But she could not live with her own treachery, and her relief was enormous when she saw Clare coming towards them.

She watched her cousin collecting glances as she walked along the quay, unconscious of the sensation she was creating, unconscious of anything in fact, except the back of Michael's dark curly head. And her smile when she joined them was the smile of a woman wholeheartedly in love.

Penny pushed her new coffee cup towards her cousin and got up. 'No, Michael, I'll fetch another one. And, Clare love, I'm terribly sorry, but I've interfered again. I told Michael you are engaged to Clive.'

The enchanted look disappeared from Clare's face, and a deep endearing pink flooded the perfect skin.

'It serves me right, doesn't it?' she said. 'Oh, Michael, I'm so sorry, I know I should have told you, but at first it was irrelevant and then later it got more and more hard to say.'

'Are you still engaged to him?' he asked.

Penny began to walk away but Clare caught her hand. 'No, Pen, stay—hear this. I *have* told Clive

106

but he won't listen—says I must wait for a few days.'

'How very sensible of him,' said Michael bitterly.

'I've told him,' said Clare in a low voice, 'that a few days will make no difference.'

'Well, I think they will,' said Penny fiercely. 'In a few days Michael will be cleared and you'll be free to do what you want. Right now if you break with Clive people will think it's because you're *sorry* for Michael.'

'I *am* sorry for Michael,' she protested.

'But you've never been sorry for Clive,' Penny expostulated. 'You've never . . .'

'Sorry for Clive?' Clare looked at her with genuine surprise. 'He's never been in a position like this. He always knows exactly what he's doing and why he's doing it.'

'But he loves you.'

'He did,' said Clare.

Penny turned away. 'Well if you've told him, you've nothing to worry about,' she said. 'This thing is bigger than both of you.'

'Penny,' Michael caught her by the shoulders. 'We *do* have something to worry about. We have Clive. Clare *is* worried; if she hadn't been she would have told me about him days ago. But I promise you, this happened so fast we neither of us knew what had hit us.'

She nodded. 'I know. I *do* know. But Clive . . . Oh well, I'll go and get my coffee.'

*I need it* she thought with a grin as she went into the café. *I'm still suffering from shock.*

As soon as she had drunk her coffee she left for

King's View. She needed to think. And as for Clare and Michael—they barely noticed her going.

But there was no time for thinking. Maria greeted her with relief.

'Do you know where Clive is? There has been an urgent phone call for him.'

'Superintendent Marshall?'

'No—from London.'

'Gosh!' Penny looked suddenly alarmed. 'He's gone to Stu's boatyards. Perhaps we could trace him.'

Maria, whose predominant feeling about the authoritative-sounding voice on the telephone had been irritation, was slightly taken aback by this re-action. What, after all, did it have to do with Penny?

Mildly, she suggested that Clive would be back for lunch and they could give him the message then.

Penny considered for a moment and then shook her head.

'I think I'd better try and find him. It might be important.'

A couple of phone calls established that Clive had left the nearest boatyard and had not arrived at the next. Penny left a message and returned to Maria, who asked casually, 'Is Clare with him.'

'No, she's down in the village with Michael.'

Suddenly Maria was tired of it all.

'Penny, what's the matter with Clare? Have she and Clive quarrelled?'

Penny sat down in a deckchair and pulled Susie on to her knees. 'No. It might be better if she had.'

'Then what happened?'

'She fell for Michael. Simple as that.'

'No, it can't be. You can't be in love with one man one day and another the next.'

'No,' said Penny slowly. 'I think it started earlier. When Clive was having his chapter of accidents he hid away like a sick animal. He wouldn't meet Clare or let her go to see him. She felt unwanted. It would probably have been all right if they could have had this holiday together but Michael came along at the wrong moment. And Michael welcomed her.'

It was all so logical, so true to character, thought Maria, that she received it with the calm of resignation. But there was a flaw in the story that made her say impulsively.

'So would Clive have done.'

Penny, who had been carefully folding Susie's soft ears over her liquid brown eyes, looked up at her aunt with much the same inquiring expression as her dog's.

'Yes,' she said simply. 'If she had ignored what he said and just gone, he would have done. But she didn't know it. And neither did he. It's funny, but it's almost as if she's frightened of him.'

Maria made an instinctive gesture of denial but the words that should have accompanied it did not come. Reluctantly she had to admit that there was a grain of truth in what Penny said.

'In awe of him perhaps,' she said cautiously.

The trouble was, she reflected, that Clare, modest to a degree about her fantastic looks, had an even lower opinion of her own intelligence. Intellectually, there was no doubt, she was not Clive's equal; she had never been able to believe that it didn't matter.

Or perhaps it did. Perhaps he needed a sharper mind, a less biddable personality in his mate. Perhaps it had all been a mistake.

There was a short silence in which Maria endeavoured to adjust her dreams of her daughter's future. She did not really want to discuss Clare's affairs with her young niece, but she was impressed with the quiet reticence with which Penny had answered her questions. It seemed to her that the wild young Penny had grown up a lot in the last few days and now was indeed a force to be reckoned with.

And Penny registered that Maria noticed more than she showed. She had always let both girls go their own way but that did not mean she lacked understanding of their problems.

'Maybe,' she said guardedly, 'they'll get together again when all this is over.'

Well, maybe, thought Maria, but she doubted it and felt doubly bereaved. Stuart's death had saddened her; now the loss of Clive seemed almost desolating. And what of him? How did he feel, watching Michael move so smoothly into his place?

She felt she hardly knew how to face him and when she heard his car draw up in the stable yard she made no move but waited for him to join them on the lawn. So, to her surprise, did Penny. It struck her once again that her niece was growing up and felt an unexpected pang of regret for the wild adolescent who had been so abruptly replaced by this poised young woman.

In fact Penny was very far from feeling poised but she was a disciplinarian and even stricter with herself than with other people. 'Breathe deeply' you told people in hospital who were in physical or emotional distress. Breathe deeply, she told herself now. You have got to face him some time, do it at

110

once, do it calmly and he will never know that a flash of self-knowledge has made you a different person.

Slowly she unwound her long brown legs and went towards him.

'Your office called. They want to speak to you urgently.'

'Damn!' He glanced at his watch. 'Who was it?'

'Maria took the call, the number's on the pad.'

He turned without another word and went into the house. When he came back he was apologetic, but he had to leave for London at once.

'Clive, it's ridiculous. You're supposed to be on holiday.'

'This is an order,' he said. 'I'm sorry, Maria, but it's obviously important.'

'So are you,' she grumbled. 'Who do they think they are?'

'V.I.P.'s' he said with a grin. 'Never mind, love, I'll be one myself one day and *I'll* be pulling the strings.' He gave her a quick hug. 'Stop being a sullen old body and get me a few sandwiches to eat on the way, will you?'

'Go by train,' said Penny. 'It would be quicker.'

He glanced at his watch. 'Have I time?'

'Just about. I'll run you to Farmouth.'

'In your old banger? No thanks.'

'The battery's down anyway. I'll take you in your car.'

He smiled. 'I'll take *you* in my car and you can drive yourself back.'

'All right.'

He turned to Maria. 'Tell Clare and Michael, will you?'

He spoke as if they were already an acknowledged pair and her heart went out to him but his attitude was brisk and businesslike and he gave her no time to sentimentalize. With a quick kiss on her cheek he was gone.

In the event he let Penny drive. Indeed he was glad to for he could sit back and relax. She was a steady competent driver; and in love with his car.

'How did you do this morning?' she asked as soon as they were clear of the house.

'Well, I only got to two of the yards. But it seems likely that Stu had never mentioned the silent boat to his managers; he couldn't possibly have been contemplating it commercially. Which would seem to prove that it was a very personal matter he wanted it for. That's good for Michael's point of view. I saw Marshall on the way back and he says there's absolutely no evidence of any correspondence between Michael and Stuart so it looks as though Michael really did know nothing about it.'

'I'm glad,' she said and fell silent, remembering suddenly the look on Michael's face as he looked across the coffee table at Clare. It was a heaviness on her mind that outweighed even her own item of unwelcome knowledge. She wondered if she should tell him what she had remembered but when she glanced at him she saw that he had apparently fallen into a doze and with relief she decided to keep the knowledge to herself. It could even be that she was wrong; why worry him, when he could do nothing about it?

Just before they reached the station he opened his eyes suddenly and said: 'You can use the car while I'm gone.'

'I suppose you will be coming back? They're not sending you on a job?'

'I don't think so, it didn't sound like that. They were a bit cagey.'

'So you're not sure?' she said.

'You can't be sure of anything in my business.'

'No, I suppose not. Well I'll bring the car up if you find you need it.'

'Thanks Penny. I'll try to keep in touch.'

She nodded. 'Do.'

But when she had driven into the station yard and parked, she said, without looking at him, 'If you don't *want* to come back, Maria will understand.'

He leant over the back seat and lifted his case. 'I've unfinished business here.'

As he turned back to open his door he caught a glimpse of her face and said gently, 'Stu's business. I know my own is finished, if that's what you're trying to say.'

She turned her head sharply away and stared fixedly at an advertisement for Sunny Penzance.

'Yes, that's what I'm trying to say. I'm sorry. I shouldn't interfere.'

'That's not interference, that's a friendly warning. Not necessary. Look at me, Penny.'

Slowly she turned her head, and he smiled at her.

'It's all right, Pen. I've come to terms with it,' he said.

But at what cost she thought. His was a face that showed everything—the frustration, the exhaustion, the misery of the last few days were all there to be seen, ruining a face that was normally a relaxed and pleasing one. And Michael had a face, she thought, with sudden illogical fury, that even when he was under suspicion of murder only went a little paler under the tan, a little tighter at the already tight jawline. His was a face that was stronger, even more handsome under strain. Clive's face, giving itself away, must be a disadvantage in a job like his.

She raised a smile that belied the look in her eyes.

'I haven't,' she said.

'You will. They're very well matched.'

He began to get out of the car and then turned back to her.

'And Michael's not to blame, you know. The damage had been done before only I hadn't realized it.'

She nodded, 'I know.'

'And once we really have proved Michael's clear of any suspicion I can even find it in my heart to wish them well.'

'You're a better man than I am.'

'That doesn't surprise me.'

They walked slowly over to the platform together and as the train came in, she said, 'Well, catch the first train back that you can. And whatever one it is, let me know and I'll be here to meet you.'

'I will. Take care of everyone and keep your eyes open.'

He patted her on the shoulder and was gone. It was, she supposed, one better than a pat on the bottom.

.        .        .        .        .

Driving back to King's View Penny made a decision. She would go out to King's Rock on her own. It would have been better to have had Clive with her but, as there was no knowing when he would return, she felt justified in going alone.

114

Taking time only to snatch up a picnic lunch she returned to the cove and to Blanes' boat. Somewhat to her relief the old man had gone out on a shopping expedition so she did not have to confess that she was going to the island. With Susie as passenger she made her way across the sunny stretch of water towards the dark heap of rock that had been Stuart's kingdom. It was the first time she had been there since his body had been found.

She tied the boat up carefully to the wooden landing stage and jumped out on to the Rock. Susie was already ashore and scrambling up the rock towards the ruin of the old house. Penny took the steps that had been cut years ago and which now led to the wooden veranda Stuart had built out from the old house.

It was a little eerie even in the brilliant morning light, for it was so exactly as it had always been. No shadow had been cast by the violent, unacceptable death of the owner of this romantic island; no sense of doom spoilt the utter peace of gently lapping sea and clear sky and wheeling sea birds. It was the same small private world that Stuart had loved so much and shared with so few. Penny had been one of those few. Now for a time it seemed to belong to her, and her alone.

In the pocket of her shorts she carried a bunch of keys. In her hand was a torch. In her heart was a certain awful fear.

She knew what she was going to do and she was not at all sure that she should be doing it.

Two of the old rooms had been rebuilt and made habitable so that Stuart could come here in all weathers. The larger of the rooms had a vast window, enabling the occupants to look out in three directions: to the ocean in front, towards Merrynmouth Point on the left and Manntor to the right. The veranda was wide enough to sun-bathe on, long enough to permit one to fish from one end of it. There was no electricity but oil lamps and heaters had been kept in order by an assiduous Blanes, who had also maintained a small store of food and drinks.

The smaller room was a store room where supplies, fishing tackle and spares for the boats were kept. It was to this room that Penny went.

In one corner there was a cupboard built into the old stone wall of the room.

She had to try several of the keys before she found the one she wanted.

It was to all appearances a perfectly normal cupboard into which you could walk quite comfortably, and it was shelved all round.

Years ago when Penny had first spent her holidays at King's View, Stuart had won her affection for ever by taking her on a personally conducted tour of King's Rock. And he had shown her the secret of the store cupboard—that it was not a cupboard at all but a stairway to the cellars of the old, now ruined house.

'Dungeons?' Penny had asked, her eyes round, her imagination wild.

'Wine cellars and cold storage for food more likely,' Stuart had said. 'You see when the tide's right you can deliver direct to the door on the sea side. That would have saved them humping stuff up the rock steps.'

Penny had preferred to think of wrongly imprisoned heroes being rescued by friends in small quiet boats at the dead of night. But now she could as easily visualize the secret receiving of smuggled goods.

But did it still work? Stuart had had the sea door blocked up so that you could not recognize it from outside and it may be that there was no longer an entrance there at all. He had, however, shown her how the cupboard door could be opened and let her look down into the cellar below.

Now she moved aside a couple of coils of rope and exposed the lock. After a few moments she found the right key. The door, heavy with its neatly stacked shelves, opened slowly but easily, and there below was the darkness of the cellar. It did not smell musty, there was no dust on the door jamb. The cellar had been used recently.

With a small sigh, Penny relocked the door, put back the rope, relocked the outer door and went back into the sea room. She knew now that she could keep the secret of King's Rock no longer; in the absence of Clive she must tell Superintendent Marshall.

She took one last look at the sea room where she had so often read or worked or simply sat gazing out at the sea and imagining herself the owner of this fairytale spot. Now it would belong to the cousin from Spain and he would almost certainly sell and there would no longer be Kings of King's Rock.

The place still looked used, familiar, untouched by tragedy. And it was very quiet. Except for the ticking of a clock.

It was on the small table beside the cushion-covered divan. It was a small clock, gilded,

117

enamelled and quite beautiful. It was out of place in the functional, masculine room.

She picked it up and left, Susie at her heels.

.　　　.　　　.　　　.　　　.

Superintendent Marshall was not available at his headquarters. He had, she was told, by a rather white-faced young constable, been called away very urgent. No, he didn't know when the Superintendent would be back.

Well, it could wait. Meanwhile she could make use of her time. She went along to the village's only garage and asked them to collect the battery of her old car for recharging.

On her way back she passed the gates of the big white house where Rowena and George Carter lived.

A huge car was parked in the short drive and Rowena was just putting something in the boot. She greeted Penny with the enthusiasm of a woman thrown too much upon her own resources—resources which in Rowena's case Penny guessed to be limited.

'Penny, you're just the person I wanted to see.' She came down to the gate, almost impossibly elegant in a white trouser suit. 'I've been having a turnout and there are some books I thought you might like. Do come and look at them.'

Penny hesitated at the edge of the pristine and polished garden. She did not really want to go in but it seemed childish to refuse and she was reluctant too, to stay overlong with her own thoughts. They were unusually disconcerting.

118

She followed Rowena into the house, feeling a little uneasy at the slight air of suppressed hysteria that still emanated from this friendly but somehow unknowable woman.

'I haven't seen you since the funeral,' Rowena was talking fast and nervously as if to round an awkward social corner. 'Gruesome, wasn't it? I told George I didn't want to go but he insisted, he was so fond of Stuart.'

She stopped in the middle of the beautiful impersonal sitting-room that looked out over the roofs of smaller houses to the little estuary beyond. 'I thought it was brave of that young man to come. There are the books, take any you want—and Penny—there are some sweaters and things I shall never wear again. Please don't be insulted at my offering them to you.' She indicated a pile of clothes which Penny could see no woman in her right mind would take as an insult.

She picked up a white cashmere sweater and said, 'Are you really going away, Rowena?'

'Well, we're talking about it. George never gets home you know and it's a bit lonely for me. Is he still here—that young man?'

'Michael? Yes.'

'Do the police still suspect him?'

'I don't know,' said Penny, 'that the police ever *suspected* him. They only questioned him.' She held a vivid orange cardigan up against herself and looked thoughtfully into a mirror.

'Oh yes, Penny, you must have that one. It's gorgeous with your hair. Put it on.'

Penny did as she was told. Indeed it was almost irresistible.

'Yes, that's marvellous. Please have it. He's fallen for Clare, hasn't he?'

'Michael? Yes,' said Penny shortly. 'I'm afraid he has. Rowena, don't you really want these?'

'They're so hot,' said Rowena vaguely, 'and I'm tired of them. Has Clive gone back to London?'

'It won't always be as hot as this,' said Penny taking the cardigan off. 'Any day now it'll go back to being cold and damp. Or are you going somewhere warmer?'

'I'm not too sure *where* we're going. But we haven't enjoyed it here recently and George could let this place for the rest of the season so I think we'll go. Perhaps back to London. We still have a flat there.'

Penny accepted the sweaters and some of the books—almost new and some of them, she suspected, unread. She felt that Rowena wanted her to stay but had no real reason for keeping her and after more, rather desultory conversation, she made a move to leave. And it was then she remembered the tiny delicate clock in her pocket.

Taking it out, she handed it to Rowena. 'I believe this is yours.'

For a moment she was quite alarmed at the effect of her words. Rowena looked at the clock as though it were a lethal weapon. When she put out her hand it was slowly and with reluctance.

'Yes. Was it—'

'In the sea room.'

'Yes, of course, I lent it to Stu—he was always forgetting the time and it has a little double alarm. So I lent it to him till . . .'

Penny cut across her babbling with the first direct

120

lie she had told in years. 'Yes, I know. Stu told me.'
Rowena looked at her for a moment, in silence.
Then she turned and put the little clock down.

'It was kind of you,' she murmured.

'Not at all. I'm glad I recognized it.'

'I miss him so,' said Rowena. 'Don't you?'

She spoke quite calmly, socially, but behind the
calm Penny was sure was the wild cry of a woman
in love. And today, of all days, for the first time in
her young life, Penny understood and sympathized.
But something told her not to show the compassion
she felt. Some inner caution or personal reserve
warned her not to allow this agonizing little scene to
go any further.

'Yes, we all do. He was a very nice man.'

'He was the nicest man I knew. And I used him so
badly.'

To Penny, Stuart had been a sort of extra
uncle, kind and indulgent who treated her with the
deference a child-loving bachelor often shows to the
children who come not too closely into his orbit.
He had had no personal glamour for her beyond his
exotic property and she had been too young when
she first knew him to find him attractive. Any other
day she would have found Rowena's grief hard to
understand. But today she had found herself seeing
perfection in a man; a man she knew to be a perfectly normal human being. A week ago she would
have taken refuge in her youth. Now, she accepted
the responsibility of one woman for another. The
enormous distance between Rowena and herself had
been covered in one leap. But she felt that if she
offered consolation she would be acknowledging
that she knew of the affair with Stuart and the time

121

would come when Rowena would regret it. Tactfully she managed to offer sympathy without committing herself. Promising to return to collect her gifts when she had the car with her, she left.

．　　　　．　　　　．　　　　．　　　　．

As soon as he arrived at his office Clive was whisked off to a conference. Expecting it to be one held by his own department head he was somewhat dismayed when he walked into a room full of high-powered individuals from several different departments including Scotland Yard. An apology was called for and he made it without bluster.

'It's all right.' His own boss glanced at the casual clothes that were not what the Department expected of its bright young representatives. 'We're grateful to you for getting here so fast.'

Clive could not imagine why. This was the oddest collection of big brass he'd seen in a long time. Invited to sit down, he did so with some trepidation. What in God's name was coming now? Heaven forbid that they were going to cut short his leave and send him on some special mission. And if so, what?

'You were making inquiries about smuggling out of Merrynmouth?' said a man he vaguely recognized as connected with Interpol. *Smuggling!* He wondered whether they'd all gone mad or he had. This band of desk-bound gentlemen getting their sharp official teeth into *smuggling*.

He had learnt not to show his feelings. 'Out of?' he said. 'No, I'd only thought of smuggling *into* Merrynmouth.'

'But you have reason to believe that there's some activity?'

'I think there may be.' He hesitated, wondering how much they knew of his involvement with the local police.

'We are aware,' said Scotland Yard suddenly, 'of your inquiries down there in connection with the death of your friend. You think he may have been involved in smuggling?'

'Or tangled with someone who was,' said Clive.

He nodded. 'But you have no idea *what* they may have been smuggling?'

Clive shook his head. 'That's what I was hoping to find out.'

'Richards,' the man who was apparently chairing this conference put an end to beating about the bush, 'Harry Mahon has been seen in the Merrynmouth district.'

'Harry Mahon!' The pieces of the jigsaw fell into sinister, colourful place. Harry Mahon was the last of the great ambush robbers to have escaped the police. A very, very wanted man.

'You may be wondering,' said Scotland Yard politely, 'why we haven't picked him up.'

'You must have your reasons.'

'We do. We have reason to believe that Mahon is on his way out of the country. So someone must be helping him.'

'And you want to know who?'

'Don't you?' The question came at him suddenly from another side of the table, from a very high-powered character indeed.

Clive turned to him and said slowly, 'I want to know who helped John Statford out of the country

123

in April when we began to suspect he was working for the East. And I want to know who got Burns and Mackintosh away last year.'

'Yes, we have reason to believe that the man who helps characters like Burns and Mackintosh to get away is the same man who helps Goyas and Vandykes out of the country. He's not fussy about details—he'll take out people, paintings, pound notes and precious stones. He's the smuggler de luxe. We need him. We need him very badly.'

'We also believe,' said Scotland Yard with a certain amount of diffidence, 'that he operates from various different places and we've had trouble catching up with him. But the last lot of gold was believed to have gone out of Farmouth and with Mahon seen in Merrynmouth, your own inquiries seemed to fit into the puzzle.'

There was a moment's silence, till Clive said, 'I only have suspicions—hunches you might say. I have no proof and no suspects.'

'Yes.' The chairman was unperturbed. 'But now that you know your suspicions are not unfounded perhaps you can help us further. We are looking now for someone specific.'

'A man with a yacht,' said Clive slowly.

'A man with a yacht based overseas. Tunis, Gib., somewhere like that.'

'And the means of getting to it from Merrynmouth.'

'A man with a lot of power and a lot of contacts. That means a lot of money too.'

They waited.

Clive's head spun a little. Odd pieces of information flew about in his brain, refusing to settle into a pattern. Through a turmoil of thought he heard

124

someone say, 'We've got to be careful who we send in. No one whom Mahon would recognize.'

'He won't recognize me,' he heard himself say.

'No. That's why we'd like you to go back.'

He nodded.

'Superintendent Marshall must remain your contact; it's well known that you're dealing with him. We'll build up a liaison just as soon as we can, without rousing suspicion.'

'Yes,' he agreed. How soon was as soon as they could?

'You know who you're looking for?' asked the Interpol man.

'I'm not sure. I'll let you know in twenty-four hours' time. I could be wrong.'

Scotland Yard nodded, satisfied. 'We'll be in by that time. Maybe not in the village but near.'

'Be careful,' Clive said. 'It's a small place and people talk.'

'We'll be holiday-making,' he said with a grin. 'Just like Mahon is. Swimming, taking trips, the lot.'

They gave him last minute instructions. They told him everything they could. They made it clear that behind him would be an organization as vast and as efficient as could be achieved in a short time. But nobody asked what he was going to do next, who he would go after, how he would go about it. He was on his own.

.    .    .    .    .

Penny spent the rest of the day with Maria, doing odd jobs about the house and garden. She felt sorry for her aunt who was clearly bewildered and hurt

125

by Clare's behaviour but she was also sorry for Clare, who was deliberately keeping Michael away from King's View and Maria's penetrating eye until such time as she could openly and with Clive's knowledge, explain that she and Clive were no longer engaged. And Clive, Penny felt pretty sure, was determined to be present, cool and calm and ready to offer his congratulations and felicitations. Meanwhile poor Maria had to suffer the rather ominous silence of her young people. Towards evening there was a call from Clive to say he would be on the last train from London.

After a rather quiet dinner over which she and Maria had by mutual consent read books and kept their thoughts to themselves, Penny took herself off. There was still a long time before she had to meet Clive but there were things to be done: collect Rowena's presents from the White House, and try to find Superintendent Marshall.

He was still out. A little uneasy Penny headed for the café to see if Michael and Clare were there but she found only Michael's landlady in an unusual state of excitement. 'A big robbery, Pen my dear, down at Watersedge, the Lord Lieutenant's house, would you believe it? And his gardener knocked out of his senses and in the hospital, so you'll not find Dan Marshall here tonight I should guess. No, I don't know where Mr. Highstone is. He and your cousin went off to dinner somewhere. Is it all over with her and Mr. Richards then, Pen.'

'Not until she says so,' said Penny forbiddingly. 'Don't gossip, Hilda. Will you ask Michael to come up to King's View with Clare tonight whatever time they get back. It's urgent.'

126

She left more uneasy than ever, her only comfort that Hilda, bred to police work, would be faithful in delivering her message.

Now with time to kill before she set off for Farmouth, she drove the short distance to the White House and parked outside the big gates. There were no lights to be seen but this could be because Rowena was in the big drawing-room on the harbour side of the house.

She pulled the wrought-iron bell handle and listened to the chimes ding-dinging through the hall. There was no answer.

The uneasiness she had begun to feel earlier was increasing almost to fright. Rowena had said she would be in.

But she hadn't *promised*: There was no reason why she should not have changed her mind and accepted an unexpected invitation.

Telling herself she was an intimidated idiot, Penny walked along to the white-painted double garage and peered in. George Carter's car was not there, Rowena's smaller, racy one was. That meant that she was in the immediate neighbourhood; Rowena was not the sort of woman to walk back from any outlying spot late in the evening. But then, of course, someone might be bringing her back. Perhaps George had come home unexpectedly and they'd gone out together.

Despite these sensible and entirely logical arguments, Penny found herself walking down the side path to the harbour side of the house. This too, was in darkness. Now she knew she was afraid—not of any physical danger, but of what this odd silence and darkness portended. Despising herself both for her

127

fear and for prying, she peered through the big french windows into the luxurious room. It was too dark to see much but the feeling of something unusual increased. This was a house deserted; not just left by owners called away on a sudden errand, but deserted. She knew this without knowing why she knew it.

Well, it was nothing to do with her.

She turned away and walked back to the car, where Susie was waiting with some impatience. Penny climbed in beside her and sat down for a few minutes thinking.

If Rowena had been blackmailing Stuart . . . ? No, that wasn't possible. If George had been blackmailing him? No, there would have been little point in that; Stuart would have told him to go to hell. But if George had discovered the affair between Rowena and Stuart, could he have been jealous enough to kill? Just possible perhaps, but not likely. George, thought Penny, was more likely to take revenge in some more subtle form. And anyway if they—or one of them—had had anything to do with Stuart's death why wait for so long and *then* disappear. Why not go at once before the evidence began to pile up? Or stay and brazen it out: running away now was more incriminating than staying. If they *were* running away. Because, of course, she had no proof, only a sort of instinct.

Perhaps they had some idea that the wind of suspicion had begun to blow in their direction. But had it? Superintendent Marshall had never shown any interest in them, at least none *she* knew of. It was only herself and, to a lesser degree, Clive, who had thought there was any connection between Stuart's death and Rowena Carter. Perhaps they'd seen *that* and guessed it would only be time before the police were on to them ... perhaps.

'Blast,' said Penny suddenly to Susie. 'Hell and damnation!'

Of course they had got wind of her suspicions— she had brought back Rowena's clock from King's Rock. Rowena must have taken that as a warning.

As if I'd warn her, she thought angrily. As if I'd warn *anybody* if they'd murdered someone.

But Rowena might, said a small cold voice. Rowena was the sort of woman who might easily believe it was better to warn a friend than betray her.

Betray—hell! You did what was honest and right. *Supposing it were Clare. Would you betray her? Or Clive, supposing it were Clive?*

'Oh hell, I don't know,' she exclaimed out loud. She hit the steering wheel viciously with the palms of her hands. I don't *know*. Yes I do. I'm not Rowena, I'm me. And it's not Clare or Clive, it's Rowena. And if Rowena killed Stuart, I *will* betray her.

*Why? The damage is done. No arrest, no trial, no punishment will bring him back.*

Perhaps it wasn't Rowena, perhaps it was George. Perhaps he did it and is threatening Rowena and she should be rescued from him ...

The clock was still ticking. That's what was wrong. So unless the police had wound it up, which seemed unlikely, someone—probably Rowena herself—had been in the sea room since Stuart was killed. So it was Rowena, or George, who had been there the other night, when she had heard the motor boat out at the Rock.

129

The clock was Rowena's. Penny knew that for she had seen it months before in Rowena's living-room. So why hadn't Rowena taken it with her when she left King's Rock the other night?

*Because she was going to need it again.*

Penny switched on the engine of the car and drove purposefully down to the harbour. She parked on the quayside and walked slowly round the harbour studying intently each gaily bobbing motor boat. George's was not there.

It was time to go to Farmouth. She made one more attempt to contact the Superintendent but was told that, though he had left the Lord Lieutenant's house, he was not back yet. There was no time to wait for him, she must go to meet Clive.

They greeted each other tensely and without en-joyment. He was dismayed at how much he would not be able to tell her, and she was concerned at having too much to tell him. She must not only let him know all she had discovered; she must also tell him of her own terrible lapse.

'I'll drive,' he said, climbing into the car.

He looked, she thought, more exhausted then ever but in no mood to be argued with. She had no in-tention of arguing but there was a lot she had to say. It must be said. And quickly.

'About the smuggling,' she began as he started the car, wasting no time on preliminaries. 'There is a cellar under the sea room at King's Rock. Did you know?'

He kept his eyes on the dark streak of road but she felt him stiffen beside her and knew she had his full attention.

'No. Tell me more.'

'It has two secret doors and it's been used recently.'

'How do you know?'

'I went there today.'

She heard with some surprise his sharp intake of breath.

'Penny, this isn't a *game*. What on earth made you go there on your own?'

'You weren't here,' she said simply.

'There might have been someone hidden in the cellar. Do you realize that?'

'Yes,' she said. 'But I didn't think there would be.'

'Why not?'

'Because whoever was there when Stu was killed would have been taken off by now. In the boat we heard the other night. They wouldn't have left anyone staying there with the police about.'

It was logical. The fright she had given him evaporated suddenly. This was not a defenceless Clare he was dealing with but the cool-headed Penny. There had never been anything to be gained by pointing out danger to Penny. She could see it for herself, and deal with it.

'Why didn't you tell me about the cellar?'

She did not answer him for a moment and he waited patiently. She was not dodging the question; Penny never did. She was only gathering her thoughts in order to give him an honest answer.

'Well, it never occurred to me that it was relevant until you said the word smuggling. And even then I wasn't sure it was still there. You see Stu told me he was thinking of having it blocked up.'

'Why?'

131

'He didn't say.' She grinned at him sideways. 'I suspect it was just to me he said that. I was a bit young at the time; he probably thought it was safer for me to think it wasn't there.'

'He was dead right,' he said grimly.

'He's dead now,' she said and her even young voice shook a little.

'O.K.,' he said after a moment. 'You *hoped* to find it blocked up. You don't want to think that Stu was smuggling. Neither do I, but it looks as though he must have been.'

'Yes, I know,' she said reluctantly.

'Why didn't you tell Superintendent Marshall?'

'I tried to but he's been at Watersedge all day. Somebody knocked out the Lord Lieutenant's gardener and then robbed the house.'

He muttered an exclamation and she looked at him in surprise. 'Clive, do you think there could be any connection between this—and Stuart?'

'Yes,' he said grimly. 'I do.'

She heard the pent-up fury in his voice and felt the big car's speed increase. She felt a sudden flash of sympathy for Clare. This could be a very frightening man—if you didn't understand him.

'There is one other thing,' she said evenly. 'I believe that Rowena and George have gone.'

She was totally unprepared for his reaction. Pulling the car into the side of the road he stopped and sat for a moment staring at the road in front of him, a set grim profile a thousand miles away from her.

Then, rubbing his hand over his face he said calmly, 'You got there before me. Tell me all about it.'

132

While he listened in perfect silence she told him
of her visits to the White House and of its closed
emptiness the second time.

'So whatever's going on,' she concluded, 'I think
they may have been in it. So they've got out.'

'Yes,' he agreed. 'I think so too.'

'But Clive, I did it. I frightened them away taking
that damn clock back.'

'You may have precipitated it,' he said, 'but they
were on their way without your help.'

She said with surprise, 'You sound very sure. I
thought you'd tell me there's no proof.'

'There isn't,' he said wearily. 'But yes, I'm sure
you're right.'

'But Clive what are they up to? George is rich,
he can't need to smuggle.'

'Perhaps he's rich *because* he smuggles. There's
smuggling and smuggling, you know. It's not brandy
and lace any more.' She was silent for a moment
digesting this. He took off the brake and began to
drive off again. The roads were almost deserted now
and miles slipped away beneath them, the quiet
night exaggerating their uncomfortable, flamboyant
thoughts.

'You mean smuggling *out*, not in?' she said at last.
'Stolen things.'

'Yes.'

'George!'

'We don't *know* George is in it, do we? But as you
said he's not likely to be in anything for peanuts. I
reckon he's an all-or-nothing man. And what do we
really know about him. He's in business. What business?'

'Property,' said Penny, and added after a moment,

'other people's property? What are you going to do?'

'Get back to Merrynmouth as soon as I can.'

'Clive, I've been thinking. We almost *know* Stuart was having an affair with Rowena, don't we? And she has her own keys to the rooms at King's Rock. So maybe Stu didn't know anything about smuggling.'

'What about the silent boat? He tried to get that.'

'Because Rowena asked him to. She could have told him she wanted it to get to and from the Rock?' She made a question of it, not a statement and Clive moved restlessly in his seat.

'Pen, you've been doing this all along—trying to believe the best. But this is a bloody nasty business with people getting killed and innocent gardeners being knocked over the head, probably for no better reason than to keep the police occupied.'

'Stu was a victim, too.'

He sighed. 'Yes. All right, have it your own way. There is a chance I suppose that Stu was innocent. Certainly it's possible he played no active part.'

'He might have kept quiet for Rowena's sake.'

'He might. But don't pin your hopes on it, Pen. When it comes to the showdown, you may find yourself very disillusioned. Prepare yourself for it anyway.'

'You think there's going to be a showdown?'

'Yes,' he said grimly.

They were climbing the Tor now and suddenly the sea was in front of them, inky black and utterly empty. The moon was past its full and had not yet risen.

When they reached the crossroads between the

134

way to the village and the road to King's View she roused herself to ask, 'Don't you want to go and find the Superintendent?'

'I'll take you home first.'

'I want to come with you,' she protested.

He shook his head, 'Sorry.'

She said no more. It was clear that he did not want her. She was miserably aware of his changed mood; his preoccupation. Whatever had happened in London had done him no good.

They drove up through the dark lane and came to the corner where one way led to Port King, the other to King's View, and as Clive turned the car upwards a tall figure shot out from the lower lane waving furiously. Abruptly Clive braked.

'It's Michael.' Penny opened her door but it was to Clive's side that Michael ran.

'Clive, there's something going on at the Rock. There's a motor boat out there.'

'Damn,' Clive cursed softly. 'Have you told Marshall?'

'He's not available. Let's get to King's View, Clare's waiting up there in case she can see anything.'

'Where've you been?' Clive barely waited for Michael to get in before starting the car again.

'Down to Port King to see if there was anyone there. There isn't. But whoever is on the Rock came from Merrynmouth.'

'How do you know?'

'Clare and I—' he hesitated slightly, took a breath and said it again with decision, 'I brought Clare home about midnight and we went for a stroll along the cliff. We heard a motor boat coming to-

135

But it stopped on the sea side of the Rock. It must have tied up because it didn't come past on the Tor side and Clare says we'd have still heard it for a few minutes if it had gone on out to sea.'
wards the Rock from the Merrynmouth direction.
'Yes, you would,' Penny nodded.

They had arrived at King's View and Clive pulled up outside the garage.

'There's Clare,' Michael started towards her as she came silently across the dark grass. 'Did anything happen?'

'No.' They were speaking in low voices, conscious of how clearly sound would carry over the quiet darkness. 'But I think there's a yacht at anchor just behind King's Rock. I thought I saw a flicker of light, but it's hidden behind the island and you can't see it from the cliff at all.'

'Can a yacht get in as close as that?' Michael asked and again it was Penny who answered.

'A small one can. The water's deep there and the Rock is very sheer on the sea side just beyond the landing stage.'

'You can see the landing stage from the cliff.' Clive was beginning to walk towards the sea. 'Didn't you see anyone land?'

'You wouldn't on a dark night like this.' Penny spoke with confidence. 'And anyway the landing stage has two sets of steps. You can't see the far one, even in daylight.'

They dropped their voices lower still as they reached the edge of the cliff and stared out at the black mound that was King's Rock. There was nothing else to be seen, no sign of life, nothing to arouse suspicion.

136

And then suddenly as a tiny wind ruffled the water there was the briefest flash of a small red light; it gave one tiny almost unbelievable wink and then was gone again as the wave receded. 'Yes,' Clive let out a long sigh. 'There's a yacht there. Within fifty yards of the Rock I'd say Michael, wouldn't you?'

'Possibly less.' Michael was straining his eyes but darkness had taken over again.

'I've got to get over there,' said Clive, his eyes still on the black shape. 'What's the quietest way, Penny?'

'Swim,' she said briefly.

There was a moment's pregnant silence.

Penny was appalled at what she had said for the thought of him doing it was terrifying but there was no going back now. She had spoken the truth.

'No!' Clare said. 'You can't. Anyway why should you? They may be harmless lovers.'

'They are not,' said Clive. 'And I wouldn't be going if I could get anyone else. But someone has to.'

'I'll come with you,' Michael moved to Clive's side as if to confirm his willingness.

'No, I need you here.'

'Don't swim, Clive,' Clare begged. 'Take the dinghy. You can tie it up this side and go up the rock without using the landing stage.'

'Too risky. He might be heard,' Penny said. 'Swimming is safer.'

'But slower.'

Clive began to walk away from the cliff edge. 'Well either way I don't propose to dive off the cliff. Let's get down to Port King.'

'By the zig-zag? We could be seen,' Clare said.

He stopped. 'Clare, you don't need to come. The

fewer of us the better. But we must go by the path, we've no time to waste.'

'Then don't waste it,' she whispered. 'Let's go, the risk isn't very great in the dark.'

The darkness made the descent maddeningly slow. The dry spell had hardened and cracked the path, exposing the stony undersoil and making it slippery and hazardous. Forced into single file by its narrowness they could not talk and between the struggle to keep their balance and the sheer dangerousness of what they were doing, the tension was like a physical pain, and the relief as they reached the foot of the cliff was almost tangible. But they did not speak until they had rounded the corner of the cove into the cover of the tall rocks.

Michael turned and looked out to sea. He said, still keeping his voice very low: 'What can you possibly do out there on your own?'

'Identify them,' said Clive grimly. He was throwing off his jacket and undoing his tie. 'Get hold of Marshall *somehow*, and tell him to send a boat out.' He pulled a piece of paper out of his pocket. 'And if the police won't co-operate, ring this number and say I told you to phone and ask for help. I promise you you'll get it. Clare, get up to the house and take any messages that may come.'

'What about me?' Penny took his jacket from him. 'Are you really going to swim?'

'No, I'm going to row.'

'That's even more dangerous,' Penny protested. 'You'll be heard.'

For a moment he looked down into her upturned face. He felt an unaccountable desire to tell her he was not afraid to swim to the rock, only reluctant to

138

arrive there unclothed and therefore disarmed. He found he could say nothing except, 'Untie the dinghy, will you, Michael?'

But Penny turned away relieved. She had been wrong about Clive's worn, exhausted face; it was deceiving. Just when an opponent might think he was at the end of his rope he could pull out another one. It was the face of a man who would look beaten and wasn't. It was a first-class face for the dangerous game of deceit.

'At least,' she said softly, 'there's a bit of wind tonight. The waves will drown some of the sound.'

Michael came back. 'Let's lift her on to the water, not push her. It'll be quieter.'

'Right,' Clive began to follow him then he turned back to Penny. 'Stay on the cliff and *watch*. What you see might help the police when they come.'

Michael stopped suddenly. 'Clive, I could cover you. If I took the motor boat out the noise of it would drown the sound of the rowlocks.'

Clive hesitated. 'You'd arouse their suspicions.'

'Not necessarily. I could keep near the coast and make for Merrynmouth. I wouldn't head for the Rock at all.'

All four of them were by the dinghy now and lifting it silently up. It swayed gently on the lapping water.

'Don't use the lamp,' said Penny, 'and keep slightly to the Tor side, there are no rocks there. You can tie up in the landward rock, the one you can see from King's View.'

'Yes, I remember. Michael—'

'Yes?'

Michael loomed out of the darkness and stood in

front of him. There was no question, Penny realized with sudden dispassionate interest, as to who was in charge. Michael was awaiting his orders, and content to be taking them.

'I think if you don't mind, it *would* be a good idea to cover me. Wait till I'm nearly there and then set out, making as much noise as you can. But for God's sake hug the coast so they know you're not making for the Rock. And look innocent! Clare, what are you doing?'

Clare was pulling on an oilskin she had found in the boathouse. 'I'm going with Michael,' she said.

'Oh no,' Clive bit back the words almost before he had spoken them.

'I'll sit up close to him and he can put his arm around me. We'll be a romantic pair, too far gone to ever notice the yacht off the Rock.'

For a moment nobody spoke. The sea washed gently on to the floor of the cove, swinging the little dinghy with it. Far away beyond King's View a car growled along the Merrynmouth road and its lights flashed a brief message of reality across the distant line of trees. The wind sighed softly and it was as if they had all held their breath and let it go simultaneously.

'O.K.,' said Clive. 'But take care. And be as quick as you can. Good luck.'

Clare tipped forward and gave him a quick brief kiss on the cheek. 'And you.' She caught Michael's hand and they went together up the beach to the boathouse.

Penny and Clive were alone on the water's edge.

'Get up to King's View and call the Superintendent,' said Clive. 'Tell him where I am and where

140

Michael's going. And tell him to check up on George. He'll understand. If he's not there tell whoever is on duty to find him and say I said so.'

'I'll find him,' said Penny, 'if I have to go to the Chief Constable.'

For a moment a smile flickered across his face. 'Yes, do that. But don't let him come alone.'

She nodded. 'A raiding party.'

'Yes.' He was in the dinghy now and ready to push off. They turned their heads and strained their eyes towards the jetty, till a wave from Michael's white-shirted arm gave them the signal. With barely a splash, with hardly a creak, Clive slid out of the shallows into the great expanse of dark.

When he was out of sight Penny crossed the beach and stood at the end of the inlet. The minutes passed, the soft sound of the oars had long since been swallowed up. Now there was nothing but silence and blackness and a tension that she knew was shared by the two waiting in the motor boat under the jetty, counting the minutes.

Suddenly, violently, using all the force of the engine, they were away, shooting dangerously down to the sea, breaking furiously on to the now-dropping tide. It was a *tour de force* of aggression, the antithesis of all that Michael believed in.

The lamps were carefully adjusted to show up the boat's passengers, the engine skilfully encouraged to draw attention to itself. Violently, ostentatiously the boat skirted the cliff and headed for Merrynmouth, almost immediately turning its stern to King's Rock. And its two passengers, absorbed in each other, gave the island not a moment's consideration.

It was gone. The sound of its engine echoed across

141

the water but there was no sign of life anywhere. The bay was totally innocent.

Penny drew a deep breath, Susie appeared miraculously at her heels and they both fled in the direction of King's View.

.    .    .    .

It was unbelievably dark. The sea washing against the steep walls of the Rock covered the small sounds of tying-up. But it was a slow and painful business and even with the boat safely moored the scramble ashore was both difficult and frightening, every tiny sound like a clap of thunder. But he was on the Rock and no one had appeared.

Clive wished he were as familiar with the place as Penny was. For an idiotic moment he wished he had brought her. He could almost feel her small strong fingers in his and hear the odd abrasive little voice— 'Not that way, it looks easy but it's too steep at the top. Go to the right, it's safer.'

Well, she wasn't here and he certainly couldn't have brought an unarmed teenage girl into this kind of risk. Fortunately he had once landed with her on this side of the rock and miraculously he could still remember what she had said.

The path round the island was not particularly dangerous. Getting to it was. Once there you had to watch your step because what had once been a broad clear walk had deteriorated over the years and was now uneven and slippery. It was one thing to climb the island in broad daylight; it was quite another matter on a night like this, in circumstances like these. He kept one hand on the wall of rock beside him, the other ready to save himself if he slipped. And little by little he edged round the steep side of the island towards the more gentle slope on which the fortified house had been built hundreds of years before.

His fingers told him where he was. The rock he had been touching merged into the foundation walls of the old building. What had been natural now had the hacked flatness of man-made stone. Now he had to be more cautious still.

Here the house was an absolute ruin. The walls had survived jaggedly and stood up in points and towers like the teeth of some great animal. Further on a few survived, roofless but complete, even to an old stone hearth here and there. And further on still, on the sea side, were Stuart's two restored and rebuilt rooms, leading out to the veranda and the landing stage.

The path led downwards now towards the old cellar doors and the end of the landing stage. This was worse. The only rocks to clutch were only a foot or two above the level of the path. But if he crouched to hold them Clive found himself tilted too far forward in the steep path. It was easier to walk upright and pray he kept his balance. It also made it easier for him to look about. And more vulnerable to any onlooker. Halfway down the path he saw the yacht, standing off, as Michael had predicted, as near as possible to the rock but, in order to hide it from the mainland, anchored inconveniently far from the landing stage. Which meant that a boat had to be used to reach it.

No wonder, he thought ironically, that they could have done with the Longmore Silent.

He was crouching now, for he was visible from the yacht. Every now and then his foot slipped and he had to halt sickeningly to regain both his balance and his composure. He thought it probable that the enemy, whoever he was, would hear the thumping of his heart. But as the path descended the sound of the sea was a little nearer and towards the end he was tempted to speed, to take risks. He resisted the temptation and arrived safely on the edge of a flatter area where the fishing platform jutted out over the low rocks. He grasped the edge and swung himself under the wooden pier into the blankness below.

He was not a moment too soon, for he had barely caught his breath and begun to adjust to the extra darkness when a door opened and footsteps sounded on the verandah above him.

Another door opened. Only a few feet above his head two men met. Clive moved back against the rock face, foolishly aware that it was a useless precaution. If they didn't look under the platform he would not be seen; if they did, he would. Where he stood could make no difference.

'O.K.,' said a voice, 'all aboard that's going aboard.'

'Cellar stocked?'

'Brandy for the parson, a nice little crate of watches; it looks just as if someone has been doing some smuggling. That'll keep the police busy for a bit.'

'Right. Put the key in the store room.'

This voice was different, older, more educated, authoritative, the voice of George Carter, rich businessman, local benefactor, smuggler extraordinary.

He spoke again, slightly more loudly, evidently

calling the sea room. 'O.K., all freight dealt with. Now the passengers.'

There was a murmur, Rowena's voice unmistakably and another with an Irish accent—Harry Mahon, criminal-at-large?

There was no time to lose. Despite the dampness of the rock against which he stood, the sweat began to run down Clive's face. If he could stop them leaving the island—delay them even for half an hour, it was possible that the powers of justice, now marshalling themselves on the mainland, would overtake them. But if they left, the difficulties of catching them would be infinitely greater.

There was more movement above him, and George's voice came quite clearly through the darkness.

'Take the motor boat back to Merrynmouth and *don't use it again.* I've asked Reeves to put it on the market when he starts letting the house.'

There was more murmuring; perhaps of protest. A door closed, a key turned in a lock. Suddenly under cover of the small noises of departure Clive moved away from his shelter and was making carefully for the foot of the landing platform where the motor boat was tied up. If he could untie it and give it a shove they would be stranded till someone on the yacht could get to them with a dinghy. If he could untie it unseen and unheard, before they left.

A voice far above him said with mocking note: 'Well, say goodbye, Rowena. You won't be coming here again.'

Suddenly sharply, unexpectedly he was aware of a pain in the leg that had only just been repaired. It was so unexpected that he faltered, overbalanced and began to slide down the steep decline on the far side of the platform. And even as he fell he realized that he might still be unseen and that his only hope was to be unheard. Clamping his lips together he allowed the inevitable fall to finish—and realized that he had no hope of reaching the boat.

'God, what was that?' The Irish voice spoke sharply, much nearer this time.

'A mermaid,' George said.

'There's someone there.'

There was a silence, the longest heaviest silence Clive had ever experienced and then Rowena said, 'No, there's no one. Let's get on.'

'Yes, I agree.' George sounded grim now. 'And put that away, we don't want any more accidental deaths. Get on.'

The footsteps echoed over the wood, rang sharply on the steps. There was the soft swish of the boat being pulled in, the sounds of embarkation and then the familiar, too-noisy *put-put* of the engine. The island was silent and alone. And he knew that for the first time he had failed in a mission.

For a few blessed moments he was unaware of pain, fear, discomfort. Then he came round to hear the deeper throb of the yacht's engines, followed by the noisy swish of the power boat as it headed back to Merrynmouth.

He roused himself then to conscious thought. It seemed that he could not move. Or rather, when he tried to move, the pain in his leg was so acute that he almost passed out again. And he mustn't do that because then the police, the Customs, Michael—whoever it was that was coming, he really couldn't re-

146

member—wouldn't find him. That wouldn't matter too much in itself because he could survive till daylight, but if they didn't find him they would think he'd either been killed or abducted and that would set them all off on a murder hunt when what needed to be done was to set out after that yacht ...

Or was it? Stuart was dead and it seemed quite possible that he had been innocent; gullible and stupid perhaps but not criminal. Catching George Carter and Harry Mahon wouldn't put Stuart King back on to his little local throne. And if George and Mahon were caught, Rowena would be too and how would Stuart have liked that? And for all one could tell maybe she had been forced into her role by George who was certainly able to recognize a position of strength when he saw one. Possibly, right to the end what Rowena had done, she had done to protect Stuart.

He suddenly remembered her face when he had come back from that nightmare swim and told the others of Stuart's death. She had been horrified all right and probably the more so because she knew who had killed him. But there was no doubt that she had been fond of him too and it seemed very probable that she had run with the hare and hunted with the hounds; loved him yet needed the protection of George, the smuggler de luxe.

Poor Stu.

Poor used, abused Stu, falling foolishly, disastrously in love too late and with the wrong person.

But women were strange. Look at Clare, abandoning him for Michael without a backward look, probably never loving him as much as he had loved her and yet trying to prevent him from coming here tonight. Probably Stuart would be glad Rowena had got away, even glad that George had, because George was Rowena's security. Women were odd, there was no doubt about that. Look at Clare who didn't really like being in the thick of the action but had gone deliberately into it with Michael, while Penny had been left standing on the beach. Poor Penny, how she must have hated that . . . wonder what she's doing now . . .

. . . . .

Penny had had her first bit of luck that day. Not only had Superintendent Marshall returned to his H.Q. but he came willingly to the phone to speak to her.

He listened without interruption to what she had to say and when she had finished he said, 'Right, Miss Keats, I'll be getting down to the quay now to meet Mr. Highstone. And don't you worry we'll be out on that Rock very soon now.'

'Clive said—' she reminded him a little tentatively 'that you mustn't go alone.'

She heard what sounded like a snort down the phone. '*He* did,' remarked the Superintendent. 'But I know what he means and suddenly I have plenty of men. Mr. Richards seems to carry quite a lot of weight. Goodbye.'

She hung up wonderingly and sat for a moment by the phone. The house was very quiet, for Maria had gone to bed early. Penny was on her own where the action wasn't.

Well, she could get back to her lookout post. It wasn't the most exciting job in the world but it might

148

be useful. With Susie still at her heels she ran back to the cliff edge.

There was nothing to be seen at all. The island was in total darkness but that didn't mean there weren't lights on the other side. The yacht might still be there or it might not.

The view from Port King was slightly different and she decided to go down there to look at the island from another angle. And as, for the second time that night, she sped down the zig-zag she heard the power boat take off from behind the island, and a few minutes later saw the yacht slip out to sea.

If she had waited to question her next action she probably would not have made it. Contrary to her public image she was not impulsive and among her fellow students she had a reputation for quick but positive thinking before she made a decision. But tonight, even as she set foot on the firm sand of the cove she had thrown off her jacket and was stepping out of the shorts she wore over her inevitable swimsuit.

The water was silky, still warm from the prolonged heatwave but cool enough nevertheless to make her realize what she was doing. Oh well, how risky *was* it? The chances were that the island was clear of danger now and the only thing that mattered was to know what had happened to Clive. If he decided to come back in the dinghy, she would hear him, it would be easy enough to hail him in this sea. If he decided not to risk the treacherous clamber back to this side of the rock but to wait for help, then she would be his messenger that all was well on the mainland. And if all was not well on the island, she had to know, any risk of danger withstanding.

149

It was two years since she had swum to the Rock at night and she was entranced again by the beauty of it, the loneliness of the water, the starkness of the island looming in front of her, the odd patches of light as the sea rippled and eddied. *I promised not to do this* she thought suddenly and laughed inwardly. A fine time to remember *that*.

She did not swim straight to the island but skirted it, giving it a wide berth so that she could look at it from a safe distance. It was utterly quiet, completely dark. She swam in nearer and saw no boats tied up. Then she swam back to the Tor side and scrambled ashore, protected by the landing stage, and stood up, waiting and listening.

The sea swished gently on to the rocks, the tide was falling fast and the waves and the wind had dropped even further. The moon was beginning to rise now and later might be bright enough to see by. But not yet. For a moment she was baffled. She longed to call out but there was after all the possibility that someone had been left on the island. All she could do was begin a systematic search. But a search for what? And where?

The question was never answered. As she stood there hesitating a soft sound began to impinge itself on her. It was not a frightening noise and not a human one. It was the scrabbling of a smallish animal on hard steep rock. It was a very wet, very tired and very conceited Susie.

'Oh, Sue,' breathed Penny and kneeling down took the dog in her arms. 'You shouldn't have, I told you to wait for me.'

Susie responded in much the same way as Penny had to her own remembered disobedience. She

150

grinned widely, a wild improbable sight in the darkness.

'Well, now you're here, you can be useful,' Penny muttered. 'Find Clive, Susie. Find Clive.'

.    .    .    .    .

Clive's dog was licking his face. Since it was now several weeks since the dog had died it was a very strange experience. He opened his eyes and looked up, not into the smooth aristocratic muzzle of his own elegant labrador but into the reprehensible mass of tangled curls that Susie used for a face.

Her jaws opened and she yelped triumphantly.

'Shut up,' hissed a voice above him.

He slid away again and became vaguely aware of his wife's voice speaking to him urgently. As he wasn't married that seemed stranger still. He forced his eyes open again and saw the white wedge of Penny's face framed above him in black velvet. No the velvet was the sky. But the face was his wife's. No, Penny's.

'Clive, you *must* tell me something. Is there anyone else here?'

'No. Unless you brought them,' he said.

She giggled in relief. 'That's better. Where are you hurt?'

'How do you know I'm hurt at all? Perhaps I'm just resting.'

'That's my boy.' She had stopped whispering now and had caught hold of his wrist. 'What happened?'

'I fell,' he said bitterly. 'I just fell. Never made contact with the enemy at all.'

'Who *were* the enemy?'

**151**

'Just as you said, Doctor—George and Rowena.'

She was silent for a moment, but she was touching him with practised, capable hands.

'A Freudian slip?' she asked.

'What?' He forced his eyelids up again and they gazed into each other's eyes.

'Would you have slipped if it had been anyone else?'

He said defensively, 'They'll probably be caught. We know who they are and roughly *where* they are and what sort of yacht they have.'

'But it won't be *you* who catches them.'

'No,' he said wearily closing his eyes again with a long sigh. 'And they just *might* get away. Yes, perhaps it was a Freudian slip.' He opened his eyes and looked back into hers. 'But it's an appalling joke.'

'I think you've broken your leg,' she said by way of answer.

'So do I. And something seems to have happened to my chest.'

'Cracked ribs I expect. Very painful but not dangerous. Have you hurt your head?'

'No,' he said. 'I'm always like this.'

She ran her fingers probingly over his head. 'No, I don't think you have either. Must have fallen feet first.'

'I deliberately fell feet first,' he said with dignity.

'Clever old you. Um, you could be worse I think, but we'll have to be careful getting you out.'

'Where am I?' he asked. 'If you will forgive the cliché.'

'In the old boathouse. The roof's gone but some of the walls are still standing.' She turned and looked up at the sky. 'I think I should go and light the

152

landing stage light for the rescue party. I shan't be long. Did you hear what I said?'

'No,' he complained. 'I keep passing out.'

'Well, pass out for a bit while I go and light the place up. You can come round when I get back.'

'Suppose I don't?'

'I'll give you the kiss of life. Don't worry, I'm not going to let you go now.' She bent over and kissed him gently. 'That wasn't the kiss of life, that's just because I'm so glad you're alive and reasonably well and living temporarily on King's Rock. Susie, stay here.'

It was in fact quite a few minutes before he lost consciousness again. This time when he came round she had a lamp.

'Ahh . . . !' he murmured.

'Don't say it, or you *will* get hit on the head. Shove over a bit, Susie.'

'It occurred to me between swoons,' he said, 'that our rescuers may be a little late. If the character in the power boat ran smack into the Superintendent, there may be a delay.'

'Michael will come,' she said confidently.

'Yes.' He moved his head trying to find a more comfortable position. 'Michael will come . . .'

'Anyway, I've got supplies now. I'll give you a nip of brandy if you'll promise to stay conscious.'

'I thought that was against all the rules of first aid.'

'I'm bending them a little just for tonight. But first I'm going to make you more comfortable.'

She shifted the lamp a little and he saw she had laid a rug beside him.'

'Where did you get that?'

153

'From the sea room. And the brandy.'

'The sea room was locked.'

'Stu always kept a spare key hidden under the landing stage.'

Suddenly she went tense and her eyes dilated. 'Stu?'

He discovered he had the strength to grope for her hand and take it in his.

'Perhaps,' he said gently, 'we shall never know. But I think it is possible that he was more sinned against than sinning. I think he let himself be duped and then discovered what it was all about.'

'And so they had to kill him?'

'Yes. I think so.'

He saw her nod as if tasting the story and finding it a likely one. And acceptable. And he found he could accept it himself.

Then a wave of pain followed the relief and at once her attention was back on him.

'Don't pass out, love, I need your help to shift you a bit.'

She knelt down beside him and he clenched his teeth. She smiled at that, the lamp and the smile illuminating her face into an illusion of beauty.

'Don't worry, I won't hurt you. Just do what I tell you.'

'Now and forever,' he agreed devoutly.

Her deep throaty chuckle was as glorious as the brandy that followed. And she did not hurt him. With surprising strength and confidence she eased him into something resembling comfort, raised him so that his breathing was easier and finally slid herself bodily between him and the stone wall so that he could lean his weight on her.

'I'm too busty,' she told him seriously, 'but you may find it useful.'

He laughed. Even to himself it was an unexpected, unfamiliar sound.

Susie who had watched all Penny's movements with the quiet confidence of one who thinks they are for her benefit, gave a sigh of approval and wriggled close up to Clive. Penny moved the lamp so that the light did not fall in his eyes and they waited.

There were stars above now and the moon was beginning to flood the sky. The tide was at low ebb and the waves were only a lullaby. It was pleasant to feel a dog beside him again, snuffling lightly and thumping a tail. There was really nothing to worry about any more . . .

'Fifteen years is too much,' he heard his own voice saying out of a drowsy silence. And realized that what he had said was incomprehensible.

But he had underestimated Penny. He always had.

'That's not for you to say,' said the low beautiful —beautiful? yes beautiful—voice above his head. 'Anyway, as a matter of fact, it's only thirteen and a half. I'm older than you think.'

He tried to grapple with the situation but it slipped away from him. His head spun. When it stopped again he said, 'But you don't want to marry, you want to be a doctor.'

'Nothing, my darling ass,' said Penny into the darkness, 'will stop me being a doctor. But you can be a doctor and be married. It's not like being a nun.'

He laughed again and it hurt. 'Oh damn. How about some more brandy?'

'Only a nip.'

'Why? You're bending the rules tonight.'

155

'Yes, but before long my boy you'll be having an anaesthetic and I don't want to have to admit you've been drinking.'

He realized with wonder that she was right. In a few hours' time he'd be out of it, the long slog would be finished, the establishment would take over and for him there would be only doctors and nurses and operating tables.

But at the end of it there would be Penny.

It would take some getting used to, but there was time, there was plenty of time.

'Are you sure?' he asked, not even sure himself what he meant.

'Positive,' she said positively and he laughed again and winced and moved his head so that her positive heart beat strongly into his left ear.

And they waited—really life was very odd—for Michael to come and take them home.